BROKEN SILENCE

by
Rene Becquet

PublishAmerica
Baltimore

First printing

ISBN: 1-4137-5436-8
PUBLISHED BY PUBLISHAMERICA, LLLP
www.publishamerica.com
Baltimore

Printed in the United States of America

Dedication

For Ray:
Fratello, you helped get me through the toughest times of my life.

To Dana:
Thanks for giving me the space that allows me to write

Preface

I am haunted, haunted by memories of the past, the demons of the present and of those yet to come.

ONE

It seemed as if the sun would never rise to warm the air and take the chill out of the small stone house nestled in the hills. Salvatore, Angela, Vincenzo, and Maria all snuggled close to one another to try to stay warm. Papa Francesco put the last piece of coal into the stove before he left for work at his usual time of 4 a.m. Tending the olive groves required the keepers to work long and hard hours. The meager wages kept food on the table and bought the essentials but provided no luxuries. Papa Francesco rationed the coal as the cooler months approached. The hot Sicilian day gave way to cold nights once the sun had set.

The children would soon be up to start their day as well, tending to their chores around the house and in the fields. The goats and sheep would have to be milked and fed and the stalls of the animal pens cleaned. The milk was often bartered at the market for flour, yeast, vegetables and some occasional red meat. Eggs from the chickens provided many meals.

Mama Melina was a tall woman for her day and the children saw her as somewhat of an imposing figure. The aroma of her fresh baked rustic bread filled the air of the tiny stone house. Sundays were special in the Melina house, as Mama baked her *pasta di casa* with fresh tomatoes, olives, garlic and cheese. Her warm bread dunked in a few drops of olive oil was the perfect accompaniment to the delicious bubbling pasta she would serve.

These were difficult times in the Sicilian countryside as real money was scarce and a few futile landowners held the power. Traveling bands of thieves often roamed the countryside pilfering and ravaging small towns. Some of the landowners' family members offered protection to the communities but always for a price. Papa Francesco despised this system. "It only makes the fat fatter and the lean leaner," he would often say. Nonetheless, he collected his wage and paid his tax to Ramuno, a son of the landowner. Don Andreo owned most of the land surrounding the small town of Campobello. Some of it had been in his family for 100 years, some he bought, the rest he acquired with murderous consequences. Papa Francesco stayed because it provided steady wages and protection for his family. Younger brothers Raimondo, Stefano, and Santo had moved to nearby Agrigento, finding odd jobs as laborers. While it was not always steady work, it was far from the grasp of Don Andreo. Agrigento also provided some type of law enforcement and, while crude, it was not run by *lupara* (shotgun) toting extortionists. Sisters Vincenza, Concetta, and Angela had found some opportunity and moved across the ocean to America. Seven brothers and sisters, some who would never see each other again as their worlds would turn in different directions.

Ramuno would come to collect his protection money every week after Papa Francesco was paid. Papa would always invite him in and pour him some wine and offer bread and cheese. Ramuno was a man of small stature, despised hard work and loved his wine. He had managed to find others like him to help him in his role of local protector. The women in the town nicknamed him "*minghia teesa*" or "hard-on" because of the way he would stare down the village women and then push down on his penis when he became erect. Don Andreo had his hands full in trying to control the actions of a rebellious son who could easily upset the balance of harmony he had established in the area. Don Andreo would often say, "The devil was in the room when I planted his seed."

Papa Francesco had noticed litters of rabbits in the fields surrounding the olive groves he worked. Don Andreo did not permit any of the villagers to keep firearms, so Papa devised a very primitive trap, utilizing shoelaces carefully placed on the hillsides to trap an occasional rabbit. This provided his family with some occasional meat. Mama Melina would smear the meat with olive oil, garlic, and herbs and roast it in her wood fired oven along with some bread. Her beautiful olive colored eyes would glisten to see the look on her children's faces relishing their occasional meal consisting of meat. Years earlier she had contracted malaria and never fully recovered. She often looked frail and tired despite her tall stature. She had bouts of excruciating pain in her joints and uncontrollable chills. Despite this malady she never uttered a single word of complaint.

In the village below, the Melina family would attend mass every Sunday. All of the children had been baptized in the village church and enjoyed dressing up to attend church. As the collection plate was passed around, Don Andreo and his family would always deposit their offering with much fanfare. It was almost as if they felt they owned the church, as well. Their superior aristocratic attitude often infuriated Papa Francesco.

"They steal from the poor and then give it to back to God," he would always say. For this reason, he would rarely put any money into the collection plate. "Don Andreo has put my share in for me, previously collected," he would remark. Despite the fact he would often curse God and use his name in vain, Papa was overheard praying every night by the children.

Festa San Giuseppe (St. Josephs Day) was a big day in the village, with special *pane San Giuseppe* or St. Joseph's bread served at mass. This particular year, the holiday fell on Papa Francesco's usual payday and Ramuno informed everyone that he considered it a sin to take anyone's money on a holy day, so he would grant a one-day grace period. He would collect his money the next day without any penalty. Since Papa Francesco had to work the next day, he placed the money in an envelope and put it on the small table by the door before leaving for work that morning. He told Mama to have Salvatore, the oldest son, give it to Ramuno when he came by to collect. "Don't let that son of a whore into my house if I am not here," he murmured.

As the sun rose that morning Mama awakened the children to start them on their chores. Angela the youngest child was not feeling well and implored her mother to let her stay in bed a bit longer. Mama obliged. She told Angela she would collect the eggs and feed the chickens for her today, but it would be double duty for her tomorrow. Salvatore and the others went to the hillsides to collect the figs that had fallen to the ground after last night's wind. Mama was in the pen with the animals when Ramuno arrived early that day to collect his fees. Mama did not hear the knock on the door and Ramuno circled the house and entered the pen. "*Buon giorno, signora,*" he exclaimed. "I have arrived to pick up my stipend."

"Please wait here while I get it for you," she replied. She quickly went inside the house to retrieve the envelope containing the money. She handed him the envelope and bid him farewell. He turned towards the door and exited the pen. Mama went about her work.

Aroused by her beauty and feeling uninhibited by the lack of anyone else's presence he quickly returned to the pen. " It is because of my protection that your beautiful eyes can shine so brightly, eyes as green as the olives in the grove," he said as he slowly approached her. She turned to go around him so as not to be trapped into the corner. He grabbed her from behind pressing himself against her buttocks and grabbing her breasts. She could feel him becoming erect as she struggled to pull away.

"*Basta, basta!*" "Enough, enough," she screamed. Angela who was sleeping was awakened by the commotion and ran to see what was wrong.

"Mama," she cried now seeing the struggle that was taking place. Hearing the little girl scream,
Ramuno quickly turned and left. Mama began to cry; Angela ran to the hillside to get her siblings and tell them that Mama was crying. Salvatore ran back to the house and found his mother visually shaken.

"Signor Ramuno hurt mama," Angela said repeatedly. Salvatore quickly ran to the olive grove to tell Papa Francesco what had taken place. After hearing what his son had to say, both headed home quickly.

When he arrived back at the house Papa Francesco asked Mama repeatedly, "What did this animal do to you?" She told him that she did not allow him to dishonor her family. Nonetheless, Papa Francesco could not allow such an action to go unpunished.

He quickly headed to the village and saw Ramuno entering a house to make his collection. Many of the villagers were in the streets as Papa Francesco approached the house. Papa began to speak to and mingle with the villagers. As soon as Ramuno exited the house, Papa grabbed him from behind and dragged him into the alley beside the house. He put a small knife to Ramuno's throat as he threw him to his back and finally pressed his knee into his testicles. Ramuno screamed in pain as Papa, pulling his hair, slammed his head into the ground violently. As Ramuno lost consciousness Papa told him, "Next time I will cut off your balls and hang them from the trees in your father's groves. I will cut out your entrails and feed them to the wolves."

Many of the villagers stood and watched as Papa Francesco headed towards Don Andreo's house at the opposite end of town. It seemed like miles to Papa Francesco before he would reach the heavily guarded perimeter of Don Andreo's house. So many thoughts were running through his head. How would he explain to Don Andreo what had taken place? How would he justify beating his son to an inch of his life? What would be the reaction of Don Andreo to his actions? It was too late to turn back. Papa Francesco felt justified in his actions, as they were to preserve the honor of his family. Surely Don Andreo would understand that his son's actions were dishonorable and not acceptable in this Sicilian society.

As he approached the front gate, one of the two armed guards who were seated stood up and lowered his *lupara* from his shoulder and into his hand. Recognizing Papa Francesco, he quickly greeted him. "*Ciao, Signor Melina*," he said. "What brings you to this end of the village today?" he asked.

" I have a personal matter, one of honor that I must discuss with Don Andreo," Papa replied.

"You know that Don Andreo does not like to be disturbed while he is breaking bread," said the guard.

Papa replied, "It is an urgent matter! I would not disturb him for a trivial matter, please grant me this favor and allow me to speak with him."

"Sit here I will go and ask for you," said the guard. Papa sat down as the guard headed down the walkway to the villa. Papa Francesco rubbed his hands together as his palms began to sweat and he nervously began to tap his feet. Through the well-manicured gardens he could see the guard approach the terrace where Don Andreo was seated. After a brief conversation, the guard once again turned down the walkway back to the gate. As he approached, Papa Francesco stood up.

"He will see you, but only for a moment and only because he regards you as one of his best workers," said the guard.

"A thousand thanks to you," replied Papa.

"First, I must search you, then I will escort you to the terrace," said the guard. As they walked down the walkway Papa grew more anxious. He could feel his heart pounding and a sweat breaking on his forehead. There was no turning back now. Papa kept wondering how would this man react to what he was about to tell him? As he approached the terrace he could see the groves where he worked on the other side of the terrace and wondered if he was ever going to work there again.

"How is it you are not tending to my olives today?" asked Don Andreo.

"With all due respect, sir, I have an urgent matter to discuss with you and then you can be certain I will make up to you the time I am away from the groves," Papa said. "You are here so speak your piece as my meal awaits me," said the Don.

"Don Andreo, as one of your loyal and faithful workers I ask that you sympathize with that which I am about to tell you. I am aware of a man in this village that has attempted to bring dishonor upon a certain woman and her family by trying to force himself upon her. So many of us in the village have nothing but our honor to call our own in life and this was attempted to be taken from one of us. How then would Don Andreo, who is so widely respected here deal with such a matter? After all, do we not all believe that no one should eat from our plate?" Papa asked of Don Andreo. "We turn to you for your wisdom and guidance," he said.

Don Andreo rushed to his feet. "He should be thought a lesson, and his balls should be cut from him and hung from the posts in the market square for all to see. Women and children should never be trampled upon by we men, for they are the weaker animal that God has placed on this earth," Don Andreo remarked. "Bring this man to me and I will make a spectacle of him and then all of Sicily will know that Don Andreo is a just person who looks after his fellow man. Bring him to me before the sun sets today and I will give you your justice! I give you my word on this and the word of Don Andreo is as good as all the gold in Sicily! Now go, as I am hungry like the wolf and would like to enjoy my meal."

"Many thanks for your time and understanding," Papa Francesco said as he turned and left the terrace.

Word of what had happened spread quickly throughout the town. Ramuno had decided to stop at a friend's house to clean himself up. While he was there he indulged in a bit too much wine and found himself in a drunken stupor. As he walked the streets and alleyways, he was yelling out loud saying that this woman had rejected him and that no woman rejects Ramuno. "Who does this peasant think she is, that she can resist one as handsome as me," he cried aloud. "I take what I want and when I want it," he continued to yell out loudly. At this point in time, many of the villagers began to laugh at the sight of this man beaten and bruised and now so drunk that he could not find his way home. As he stumbled in front of the church, Father Licata the local priest noticed him. With the help of some of the men who were outside at the time, he loaded Ramuno into a hay wagon and headed towards Don Andreo's villa. Stopping at the gate, he informed the armed guards that he had Ramuno in the wagon and would like to get him inside. The guards allowed him to pass and informed Don Andreo. Don Andreo met the priest and the wagon once inside the villa grounds.

Father Licata told him of what the people in the village were talking about and what Ramuno had been saying. "It appears that your son has transgressed the honor of another man and has paid a heavy price for his actions. I will hear his confession in the morning and ask God to forgive him of this sin," Father Licata said. Ramuno was helped to his feet by some of the attendants in the villa as his father approached him.

"Ramuno, is it true what Father Licata has told me, that you have attempted to bring dishonor to another man by taking his wife?" asked Don Andreo.

"Of what concern is it of yours my dear father? I am free to put my dick wherever I please because I am the most feared man in Sicily, now please allow me to lay in my bed as I have some business to finish tomorrow."

Don Andreo was so angered by his son's words that he slapped Ramuno across the face and spat on the ground in front of him. "Even the most powerful of men must conduct themselves with dignity," Don Andreo replied. He then apologized to Father Licata and thanked him for bringing his son back home. At that moment he recalled the earlier conversation he had with Papa Francesco and now realized that it was Ramuno that Papa Francesco was referring to.

It was not the first time that Ramuno had put Don Andreo in an embarrassing situation as this one and each time his patience waned. But what now was he to do of the promise he had made earlier? Was he to cut out his own sons testicles as he had promised or was the revenge that Papa Francesco had already taken out on his son enough? He decided to wait and see if any inquiries would be made from Papa Francesco and hoped that the matter would be closed. Although Don Andreo was a powerful man, he feared an uprising amongst the locals could challenge his position as the local Mafia leader. He tried to be fair to all the local villagers and avoided instigating them. He had won their trust and it had been ten years since a power struggle had brought him to power. These power struggles always ended in bloodshed and he sought to avoid this at all costs. He had become complacent in his role, but understood that a well-planned conspiracy against him would cost him not only his position, but his life as well as those of his family members. A Mafia leader always walked a fine line between allegiance from his subordinates and an act of betrayal.

TWO

Sunday had arrived and the Melinas were headed to church as they did every Sunday. They arrived at church and noticed that Don Andreo and his family were not present as they usually were. Papa and his family sat in their usual places as they listened to the mass being said. As Papa sat in the pews, many thoughts filled his mind. He was torn between making a confession for his actions against Ramuno and feeling justified in what he had done. "God will understand," he thought to himself. Papa was a God-fearing man, but in Sicily there was also a code that all Sicilians were indoctrinated with.

The Catholic Church with its many influences, set a moral standard for all men to live by, but here much more was needed. These codes formed the basis for survival. Often times, one's survival meant another's demise. Life existed in a rather fragile state in a world dominated by powerful men. The Holy Roman Empire was still alive here in a small way, each town having its own Caesar backed by his legions. One thing that will never change in this world is that power, while held in the hands of the few, will always eventually corrupt individuals and lead to the demise of an entire civilization. It was no different here as has been the case throughout all of civilized history; one powerful civilization will always replace another. This was usually done at the expense of those not wielding the power and it was often the common man who paid the price with his own blood.

The collection plate was passed in its usual manner and Papa felt compelled to make a donation. Was it from the guilt that he felt over almost taking a man's life or from the lack of presence of Don Andreo's family? He reached into his pocket, pulled out some loose change and placed it in the collection plate. He turned and smiled at Mama Melina and winked at the children. Now he felt better about himself and his family and remained a member in good standing in the Catholic Church. ACTIONS JUSTIFIED! Just as the mafia dons will buy allegiance through blood or money, so too had Papa justified his actions by his presence in God's house and his contribution to the poor. It was as if he had bought Gods approval. Papa turned to Mama Melina and whispered in her ear, "Today is a good day. God is happy we are here."

He turned his attention to the priest who was concluding his sermon. The last words he heard the priest say were, "God blesses us all in his own special way." Papa thought to himself how blessed he really was, perhaps not in a material sense, but in a spiritual sense. The things in life that were truly important he knew were his. A loving wife, beautiful children and the honor of his family, all of which he held so dear.

As they left the church that morning they headed back to their home along a road that paralleled the olive groves. The road, like most, was a narrow dirt road, slightly elevated from the rest of the terrain. Papa chose this route so he could check the rabbit snares he had placed on the hillsides. A rabbit today would be the perfect compliment to the meal Mama Melina was preparing. He felt confident as he walked down the road that today he might even find two rabbits. A tremendous feeling of well being had been with him all day and he felt a sense of tranquility as he had never felt before. "Wait here with the children," he said as he descended the gradual slope along the road. Mama, with Angela in her arms, watched him, as he seemed to disappear, descending further down the slope. She turned her attention to what seemed to be the sound of a horse neighing in the distance. Just as she turned, she heard a loud blast from the slope and felt a stinging warm sensation in her arm. In an instant as she reached with her hand to feel the warm trickling sensation in her arm, she saw a puff of smoke coming from the trees. She could hear a loud moan from where Papa had descended the slope.

"Rita, Rita, help me."

She now realized that it was Papa moaning and calling her name. She saw the blood trickling down her own arm and she could now hear the cries of her frightened children as she suddenly began to realize what had taken place. She quickly led the children down the opposite side of the slope so to offer protection from any more shots that might ring out. She raced back up the slope onto the road and down the opposing slope to look for Papa. It seemed as if her heart was beating in her throat as her pulse quickened. As she looked down and saw Papa's lifeless body, she began to scream, "No, no, no!"

How could this be happening? she thought. *It must be a bad dream.* As she approached her beloved husband, she could see him grasping the small hand-carved wooden cross he wore around his neck. She realized it was too late.

She slid down alongside him and slid her arms under his lifeless body and pulled him close to her. The blood from his clothing now penetrated her clothing as she began to weep even harder. She rocked him in her arms as a mother would rock a baby to sleep.

"They have killed my husband, sons of whores, bastards. Who did this to this man?" she cried aloud. "Francesco, who was it, Francesco? Why, Francesco, why?" she cried.

As she looked up, she now noticed her children standing at the top of the road. Salvatore who was holding Angela by the hand was staring piercingly at his mother. He could see his father's blood smeared on his mother's cheek. While he could not fully understand what had transpired, he realized that his father was no longer alive. Mama Melina could now see the fear in her children's eyes as she noticed all of them standing by the road.

All the children led by Salvatore, now descended the slope to where Mama was. They all knelt down beside her and began to cry, as well. Little Angela broke away from her brother's grasp and threw herself on her mother. "Don't cry Mama, don't cry," she said. Turning to her brother Salvatore she said, "I want to go home, I want to go home, take me to my house."

As the broken family huddled together on the slope beside the road, a donkey and carriage approached. It was Fillippo Vittelaro who worked in the groves with Papa and often ate lunch with him. They would find a shaded place under a tree and break bread together. Their lunchtime meals consisted largely of fresh bread, green olives some cheese and oil for dunking their bread. They shared their dreams of someday finding a better life for their families and hoped the luxuries of life that had somehow passed them by would find their way into their children's lives. Fillipo, the father of eight children, had known Papa for several years. At one point in time, he had gathered several of the villagers to discuss the overthrow of the Andreo family.

Because it would ultimately involve the assassination of several individuals Papa was opposed to the idea. "Bloodshed leads to more bloodshed," he told the assembled group. "What would we have to gain that we would not ultimately lose at some point in time, and at what cost?" Papa felt that whatever he could give to his family had to be acquired through hard work and not at someone else's expense. He treated others as he would expect to be treated and was always fair in his dealings with others. For this reason, many people often sought Papa's counsel and advice. They knew he was level-headed about matters and could be counted on to always find a compromise to head off any potential conflicts.

As he approached the groves, Fillippo could now see the Melina family huddled alongside the road. As he looked closer, he saw the children crying and Mama Melina crouched next to Papa.

He brought the donkey and carriage to a halt and jumped off the carriage. He hurried over to where Papa was lying and could see from the morbid expressions on mama's and the children's faces that something terrible had taken place.

"*Dio mio, Dio mio*, my God, my God. What has happened?" he asked.

"They have killed my beautiful Francesco," cried Mama.

"Who did this?" asked Fillippo.

"The bastard Ramuno," Mama cried.

"Did you see him?" asked Fillippo.

"Who else could it be? Only Ramuno could it be," she cried.

Fillippo took the children by the hand and led them to the carriage. He then went back for Mama and had to pry her away from Papa's lifeless body. After loading them all in his carriage, he headed back down the road to his home where he left Mama and the children. With Mama and her children now in a safe place, he headed back to the place where Papa's body still laid. Along the way he stopped to ask the assistance of some of the village men whom he had seen out and about earlier. Two of them offered to assist in loading the body onto the carriage.

Word quickly spread through the village of what had taken place. All of the suspicion now turned to Ramuno because people knew that the Melina family had no other enemies. The questioning soon turned to talk of the vendetta that would take place once the brothers of the victim received word of his demise. Fear grew that the small quiet village would once again be gripped by murderous vendettas that had earlier claimed half the men of this village. To a Sicilian, the only form of true justice is a vendetta.

The Mafia dons controlled the local governments to a large extent. The Italian government in Rome had, for many years, attempted to curb the powers of the Mafia by imprisoning large numbers of villagers for conspiracy and other crimes. Each time another boss would emerge and the provinces would have a new mafia leader. Since Sicily was considered to be a poor land and held little political power or influence, the authorities in Rome chose to at times ignore the Mafia dons and their control of Sicily. The *carabinieri,* or police, were stationed in the larger cities such as Palermo, Messina and Catania. They would never have cause to venture into the small villages and towns that surrounded these cities unless a major crime was reported to them. For the most part it was the mafia dons that held the social order together in these villages and towns. The dons also knew that any breakdown in the social order would be an invitation for the carabinieri to descend upon them and possibly take away their control over the towns and villages.

As the two men loaded the body onto the carriage, Fillippo wandered over to a patch of tall grass by the olive trees. A reflection in the grass caught his eye and he approached it carefully. As he bent over to see the shiny object, he realized it was a fired shotgun shell. He picked it up and held it closer to his eyes. He knew at that instant that it was Ramuno who had slain Francesco Melina.

The hills surrounding the village were filled with wolves that would occasionally wander into the villages seeking food. Its victims, often times, would be a chicken or a goat left unattended. This would be further invitation for other wolves to feed in the village, as well. To help curb the population of these wolves, the local leaders would organize wolf hunts. Fillippo who was renown as an expert marksman would often accompany the hunt parties. He had noticed on the last hunt that Ramuno had loaded an unusual brand of shotgun shell into his gun. It was one that he had never seen before and he commented on it to Ramuno. "They are from America, a gift from my cousin who visited there recently," Ramuno remarked.

"Remington," Fillippo recalled. It was the same brand he was now holding in his hand. "God have mercy," he whispered to himself.

THREE

Vittelaro quickly sent word to the Melina brothers who were in Agrigento. The bearer of the tragic news was Mario Rilado. Mario was a local carpenter who had grown up with Francesco Melina and his brothers. He arrived at the house where Stefano lived and broke the terrible news to him first. Stefano summoned the other brothers to his home so he could share the news with them. All three agreed that this act must now be avenged and they felt that the evidence Vittelaro had found gave them their suspect.

It was agreed upon that as soon as the word spread that Ramuno was behind the murder, the Andreo family would be awaiting the next move by the Melinas, most likely a vendetta. To act now or even make themselves noticeable would be suicidal, since Don Andreo would likely have them all killed before they could retaliate. It was decided to lay low and wait for the appropriate time to seek revenge. Raimondo would have the task of taking out Ramuno, but the other members of the Andreo family would have to be eliminated, as well, to avoid more retaliation.

Raimondo also feared that Don Andreo would murder his nephews, Salvatore and Vincenzo, to avoid any acts of vengeance, as they grew older. For this reason, he arranged for his sister-in-law, nephews, and nieces to be brought to Agrigento.

Back in Campobello, Don Andreo received word of the killing. He, too, suspected his sons involvement. He sent his bodyguards out to look for him. Later that evening they found him at the home of a young widow where Ramuno frequented. It was ironic that Don Andreo had killed this woman's husband for stealing a wagonload of olives, and now she would be Ramuno's whore. The bodyguards escorted Ramuno back to the villa where Don Andreo awaited his return.

As he approached Ramuno, Don Andreo began to question his son. "There is news that Francesco Melina was shot dead earlier today," Don Andreo said to his son. Ramuno said nothing to his father as he stared him directly in the eye. "I would like to think that you were screwing your whore all day, but my senses tell me otherwise. Surely that would have been the lesser of the two evils," Don Andreo said to him. Again Ramuno said nothing. " I will see to it that the servants say you were here in the villa until you left to visit your whore if any inquiries are made."

" I do not need for you to do anything for me," Ramuno replied. "Who in this town is willing to challenge our authority? Why do you fear these peasants?"

"It is not the so-called peasants I fear, but the war that you will bring upon us if others were to know," quipped back Don Andreo.

"Fuck them! We should kill them all before they can get to us," said Ramuno.

"And then are you forgetting the *carabinieri* that will descend upon us when news of a vendetta reaches the city," responded Don Andreo.

Don Andreo walked away from his son, contemplating what his next move should be. He felt as though he could kill him with his own hands for what he had done. He knew in his heart that no matter what fabricated story he could provide, there would be no convincing others of it. It was only a matter of time until the Melinas would come seeking revenge.

Fearing retaliation, Don Andreo made arrangements to have bodyguards escort Ramuno wherever he went. Don Andreo rarely left the villa in the weeks after Francesco Melina's death and he was constantly making inquiries as to the whereabouts of the Melina brothers.

Six months had passed since the murder of Francesco Melina and Ramuno had become boastful in his inner circles about his ambushing and killing of Francesco Melina.

Don Andreo had contracted pneumonia and was confined to his bed for several weeks. The knowledge that six months had passed and there was no sign of the Melinas had given the Andreo clan a sense of security that perhaps the Melinas were not going to retaliate after all. Perhaps they had grown complacent in their life in Agrigento and were not willing to risk what they had. As time went on, the Andreo's tended to let their guard down a bit and his bodyguards no longer accompanied Ramuno wherever he went.

It was a Friday morning and Ramuno had started his day by visiting his whore for some early morning pleasure. He did not notice the crouching figure outside the window as he entered her home. As he was having intercourse with her, he boastfully said he would be back to screw her again after collecting his protection money for the week. He told her to have some wine ready as it was his birthday and she could suck his dick as a birthday present. He left about an hour later, never noticing the man crouching outside the window. He headed out to make his usual rounds collecting his protection monies.

Back at the villa, Don Andreo had summoned the doctor as his condition deteriorated further. After examining Don Andreo, the doctor left telling the caretakers that he would mix up an elixir and have it sent to the villa later that afternoon. What Don Andreo did not know was that one of his gate guards was relaying information to the Melina brothers, who had arrived in town secretly the day prior.

As the day wore on, Ramuno was finishing up his rounds. He arrived at his last house to make his collection and entered the house. He noticed that just up the street was a horse and buggy parked with what appeared to be two monks from the nearby monastery. Ramuno thought nothing of it. After a few moments, he exited the house and mounted his horse to travel back to the villa. As he began his mount, the two monks in the buggy approached him.

"Good day," one of the monks greeted Ramuno.

"Good day to you, too, and what brings you to town today? Did you forget to buy flour for your bread?" joked Ramuno.

"We have come here to pray that mercy might be granted to a soul in this town before he enters the gates of hell," responded one of the monks.

"I am not so certain I understand what it is you say," Ramuno said with a quizzical look on his face.

"One thing is for certain," the monk said as he threw off his cloak and raised a *lupara* towards Ramuno. Ramuno now realized this was not a monk but Raimondo Melina. "You will not see my brother where you are going."

At that instant Raimondo pulled the first trigger, sending a blast towards Ramuno's chest that sent him hurling off his horse and onto the ground. He then dismounted from the buggy and pulled the second trigger, hitting Ramuno directly between the eyes. The corpse was now a mangled, bloody mess and unrecognizable. There was a gaping hole in the upper torso and the face was blown completely away. Raimondo pulled out a knife and cut off Ramuno's trigger finger. He then cut off his penis and carried both body parts back to the buggy with him. He grabbed some rope off the buggy and with the help of his brother, Stefano, loaded the corpse onto the wagon.

They headed back towards the villa, making there way through town. When they reached the olive groves of Don Andreo, they stopped to string the corpse of Ramuno to a tree. As they neared the gated entrance to the villa, Raimondo put on a large hat that would not only cover his head but almost his entire face, as well. When they arrived at the gate, the two guards stood up to greet Raimondo who was now seated alone on the buggy seat.

"I am here to deliver some medicine for Don Andreo, I have carried it all the way from Agrigento," Raimondo said.

"I have never seen you before," responded one of the guards. Just as he approached the buggy, the other guard, who was working with the Melinas, struck him in the head with a large stone sending the guard to the ground. At that point, Stefano, who had been hiding under the straw in the back of the buggy, jumped out and plunged a knife into the neck and chest of the fallen guard. Raimondo descended the buggy and made his way onto the villa grounds. As he approached it, he looked towards the back of the house to get his all clear signal from the other guard who was working with them. He entered the house and headed directly towards Don Andreo's bedroom.

Don Andreo was sitting up and looked up at Raimondo as he approached.

"Who are you?" he asked.

"I have come to deliver your medicine, Don Andreo," replied Raimondo. "I want to tell you that this medicine will make you forget all of your health problems, it is like paradise."

Don Andreo looked puzzled as Raimondo pulled out a small sack and emptied its contents onto the bed. It was the bloodied finger of his son. Just as Don Andreo was looking up, Raimondo pulled a garrote from his pocket and wrapped it around the throat of Don Andreo. As he tightened the garrote, Don Andreo's eyes bulged from his head.

"Your son awaits you in hell," Raimondo said to him as the last breath of air rushed from his body.

Raimondo quickly headed back to the buggy where Stefano was waiting. As the buggy drove away from the villa, Raimondo once again slipped into the monk's cloak. Stefano, who was driving the buggy, headed towards the house of Ramuno's mistress. Stefano stopped the buggy in front of the house as Raimondo jumped off the buggy and entered the house. Ramuno's startled mistress jumped up from the table where she was seated to confront who she thought was a monk.

"How I can I help you, Father?" asked the woman.

Raimondo slid the small, bloodied sack across the table towards the woman.

"I would suggest you do not put this one in your mouth," he said to her as he headed towards the door.

The woman curiously opened the sack and, upon seeing the bloodied penis, let out a loud scream. As Raimondo mounted the buggy he said to his brother, Stefano, "Maybe she can put it in her soup, it is not good for anything else." Stefano drove the buggy towards the outside of town where Fillippo Vittelaro and Mario Rilado awaited them. "I have avenged my brothers death," Raimondo said to the two men.

Raimondo and Stefano dismounted from the buggy and mounted two horses that had been waiting for them. "Do not speak to anyone or look directly at anyone that you may encounter. Go quickly and be safe," Fillippo said to the brothers. They quickly headed back towards Agrigento as Fillippo and Mario took care of disposing of any evidence that may have been left behind.

Back in the olive groves of Campobello, Don Andreo's two nephews were busy in the processing building pressing olives to make olive oil. The guard who was working with the Melinas now entered the building and greeted the two nephews. "How is the pressing going today?" he asked.

Just as one of them began to respond the guard pulled a revolver, dropped to one knee and fired a shot into the chest of one of the nephews. As the stricken man fell to the floor, the second ran behind one of the large barrels that held the pressed oil in an attempt to hide from the gun wielding guard. As he tried to crawl under the iron brackets that held up the barrel, he was pulled out from his legs by the guard, who now stuck the pistol into his ass and pulled the trigger. As the wounded man screamed in pain the guard now pointed the gun to his head and pulled the trigger again. This time there were no more screams. The guard quickly dropped the gun into one of the presses and exited the building.

"An eye for an eye and a tooth for a tooth." That is what the word of God says and in Sicily that was usually translated quite literally. This little town amidst the beautiful olive groves and the warm breezes once again had its soil saturated with the blood of men, unforgiving of past sins and the atrocities committed against them. So the cycle of life and death comes full circle, accelerated by vendettas and justified by the word of God.

FOUR

Word quickly spread about the killings in Campobello. The local police authorities saddled with the widespread vendettas going on not only in Campobello, but in other small towns, as well, became very concerned if word of this breakdown of law and order reached Rome, the national authorities would soon be interfering with the social structure which had been established between the Mafia and the local police authorities.

The Mafia paid a hefty sum to local authorities to be blind to their activities in the small towns and villages which dot the Sicilian landscape. In return, it was the Mafia leaders who were responsible to maintain the peace and order. From time to time this balance got out of hand and the government in Rome would attempt to restore law and order by sending troops to regain control. This put a crimp in the activities and cash flow of not only the mafia dons but of the local police authorities who were on their payroll.

The local police chief in Agrigento was suspicious that the Melinas may have been behind the assassinations of the Andreo family members. Fearing an incursion by the National Police, he sent two of his officers to bring in the Melinas for questioning.

The National authorities way of dealing with this unrest was simply to round up anyone whose names may be mentioned as associated with any crime and throw them all in prison. There was no due process of law. One thing this action did was to get any potential lawbreaker off the street where he could not commit a crime. In turn, this created power vacuums in the mafia hierarchy and new leaders would emerge as so many others went to prison. This, in turn, would set the stage for more power struggles, as many of the jailed leaders would seek to return to power when they were released from prison.

As the two police officers approached the home of the Melinas, little Salvatore saw them from a distance. "Uncle Raimondo, look, the police are coming down the street. Maybe they can help us find the bad people who killed Papa," he said.

Raimondo called out to his brothers pointing to his sister-in-law, "Get her and the children and hide in the back room. I will talk to the police." Raimondo knew there would be no discussion, he must act quickly or he and his brothers would all be imprisoned.

As the police officers entered the small alleyway that led to the house, Raimondo lay in wait with his *lupara* by his side. Before they could round the corner to approach the house, he stepped out from behind the wall and pulled the first trigger, striking the first policeman in the shoulder. He quickly raised the shotgun to the other policeman and pulled the trigger, firing before he could unbuckle his holster and pull his pistol. The blast struck the officer in the legs and knocked him to the ground. It was now time to go into hiding.

Barely two months had passed since the killings of Don Andreo's clan in Campobello and the shootings of the police in Agrigento, when the authorities in Rome sent word to the police chief in Agrigento that Rome was ready to intervene in the situation. The police chief in Agrigento was able for a short time to convince the national authorities to let them handle the situation and that they were making progress in the search for suspects. Unfortunately, the killings had disrupted the normal course of business activity in the pressed oil business. The national government official responsible for the regional affairs in the Province of Agrigento had ties to a packaging operation that had been severely impacted by the disruption in business. He had no choice; he had to dispatch a unit of *carabinieri* to Agrigento to investigate. Unfortunately for the Melinas, this mere coincidence would set in motion life changing events for their entire family.

Ricardo Morrisso was the lead *carabinieri* assigned the task of investigating the incidents in Agrigento and Campobello. He began his investigation in Campobello. The villagers in Campobello told the officials of the chain of events that had led them to their small village. Since many of the locals were employed in the olive business, their livelihoods were at stake as long as the groves were shut down. Morrisso left a small team behind to reopen the groves and get business back on track. He then headed back to Agrigento to deal with the Melinas and the local authorities.

The Melina brothers, Raimondo, Santo and Stefano, had gotten word that Morrisso was headed back to look for them. It now became increasingly dangerous to hide in Agrigento and going back to Campobello was no longer a possibility. It was decided that Santo and Stefano would take Mama Melina and her children and head north to the Italian mainland via ferry to Reggio Calabria. There they would decide what was to be their next move. It was feared that all the adults of the family would be imprisoned and the children be sent to an orphanage when Morrisso arrived. Raimondo would stay behind to try and gather some money to relocate the family. He felt he could play a game of cat and mouse with the authorities long enough to allow the other members of the family to escape the reaches of Morrisso.

Three days had passed and Stefano and Santo had finally arrived in the seaside city of Messina to await news from Raimondo. They took refuge in the home of Signor Aldo Pugliese, a local businessman who had helped to send the three Melina sisters to America. Arrangements had been made for a place to stay in Reggio, at the home of distant relatives of the Pugliese family. Aldo himself put up some considerable money to insure everyone's safety. Aldo then sent his son Giovanni to Agrigento to find Raimondo. This would not be very difficult since Aldo had some good idea where Raimondo may be hiding out.

Giovanni found Raimondo and was given a considerable sum of money by Raimondo to take back with him. "Put them on tomorrow's ferry to the mainland. I will stay behind a few days to divert Morrisso and his men. I hope to rejoin them in a week's time. Give them my love," Raimondo said to Giovanni. Giovanni quickly returned to Messina to deliver the money and news from Raimondo.

Within 24 hours, Santo and Stefano were on their way with the remaining Melinas to the mainland. Raimondo kept Morrisso on the chase a few more days and then headed north.

Along the way, Raimondo stopped at a local mercantile to buy some cheese and bread. The clerk noticed that Raimondo's right shoe was bloodstained. The blood that splattered on Raimondo's shoes when he mutilated Ramuno had stained his shoe. The clerk asked Raimondo if he had recently butchered a pig.

"Why would you ask such a question of me?" asked Raimondo.

"I notice you have bloodstains on your shoe," replied the clerk, jokingly.

Raimondo replied, " I castrated an animal not too long ago. He bled like a pig." Raimondo turned and headed for the door and went along his journey to Messina.

Soon thereafter, Morrisso entered the mercantile to buy some wine and meat. As the clerk went about cutting the meat, Morrisso told him he had an exhausting day from tracking a fugitive, but felt he would soon have his man.

"What crime has this man that you are looking for committed?" asked the clerk.

"He killed a man and then cut off his finger and castrated him like a wild animal," replied Morrisso.

"Let me ask a question, if I may," said the clerk. "This man you are looking for what does he look like?"

Morrisso proceeded to describe Raimondo.

"Interesting," said the clerk as he shrugged his shoulders.

"Have you seen this man?" asked Morrisso.

"It's possible," replied the clerk.

"What the dick do you mean, possible, you fucking piece of poor Sicilian peasant shit?" replied Morrisso. He jumped over the counter and threw the clerk to the ground while placing his hands around his throat. "Do you think I am going to negotiate a payment for information from you? You will tell me now what you know or I will break your fucking neck."

The clerk began to speak and told Morrisso about his encounter with Raimondo

"This has to be him," said Morrisso. "It has to be." Morrisso then left without the meat and wine he had come to purchase.

Morrisso, in a rush, headed back to the police station to gather whomever he could to help him comb the area in search of Raimondo. He sent telegrams to police stations in a 100-mile radius of the town to be on the lookout for a man wearing blood stained shoes. He knew he was closing in on his suspect and it was only a matter of time until he captured him. He was confident he had left Agrigento but struggled to figure out where he could possibly be headed. He knew that in the small towns and villages it would be difficult for an entire family to travel together and not be noticed. He dispatched a small group of *carabinieri* to small towns and villages surrounding Agrigento to inquire whether anyone had noticed any strangers passing through their town. Based on the information they had gathered, he was able to surmise the general direction in which they were headed.

He asked one of the local *carabinieri*, "Where would you go if you were running from the police and headed in this general direction?" He circled the small towns on the map where the Melinas had been seen and drew an arrow through them.

"I would take the ferry to the mainland," answered the *carabinieri*.

"Why the mainland?" he asked.

"Look here… there is no work in Sicily and the towns and villages are too small to hide in. Everybody knows everybody; you don't fart here without someone knowing about it. We Sicilians are so close we could even identify who did the fart just by the smell. So you go to the mainland, to the big cities and there you don't get noticed. I bet you don't even know who your neighbors are in Rome, do you? Unless, that is, you are fucking your neighbor's wife, but then you only know her name."

"You make good sense there. I didn't think about it that way. You may have a point," replied Morrisso. "One more question…"

"What is it?" asked the *carabinieri*.

"How did you know I was fucking my neighbor's wife?" asked Morrisso. Both men began to laugh loudly.

FIVE

Stefano and Santo, along with Mama and the children, had safely reached their destination in Reggio and waited for Raimondo to join them. They hoped to find work in the port city. They could easily blend in here, as there were many Sicilians in this city. Here they would be just another face in the crowd. Since there was not much collaboration between Sicilian authorities and authorities from the mainland, they in all probability would not be looked for by the Italian police. This could be a good place for a new start.

Raimondo had begun to weave his way north to Messina and was being very careful along the way not to arouse the suspicions of the locals as he passed through each town and village. On several occasions he found a stable to sleep in, sneaking in under the cover of darkness and leaving before sunrise. He ate figs and other fruits from the many trees that grew in Sicily. Slowly but surely, he was getting closer to his destination.

One night as he lay sleeping in a stable under some hay, he was awakened by a swift kick to his feet. There he saw a man standing above him with a shotgun pointed directly at him. "Don't move too fast or I'll let you have both barrels," the gun-toting man said to him.

"Please, your forgiveness, I have been traveling and have no money and no place to sleep; I was only borrowing this space for the night to rest," said Raimondo. He continued with a grin on his face, "This space was not occupied and I think the mules in the stables rather enjoyed my company."

"What is your name and where are you from?" asked the man with the gun.

"My name is… uh… Angelo and I am from Catania. I am traveling to see my sick sister in Palermo," replied Raimondo.

"You do not make a very good liar; if you are from Catania you are headed in the wrong direction to go to Palermo," the man with the gun replied. He continued, "I am willing to bet you are the man the authorities are looking for, the one who shot the *carabinieri*."

"No, no, signor, I know nothing about any shooting. I am simply trying to get to my sister before she dies," replied Raimondo.

At that point the man put down his gun and said to Raimondo, "Come inside, my wife will prepare a meal for us; we should plan your best route to Messina. The authorities are on the alert for you and it is very dangerous. I have some ideas that may help you." Raimondo followed the man into his house. "What is your name?" asked Raimondo.

"My name is Vittorio. Vittorio Gambini," replied the man.

"I suppose you already know my name," responded Raimondo.

"I do, indeed," replied Vittorio.

Vittorio then went to his bedroom to awaken his wife and returned with her a few moments later. She greeted Raimondo as she entered the room. " Welcome to our humble home. It is very good to have you here. I will prepare some food for us."

As she prepared the meal the men discussed the stories that were circulating about Raimondo and the shootings.

Gambini told Raimondo he thought it best for him to make his way to Reggio through another port city like Catania.

"There are no passenger ferries in Catania," Raimondo told Gambini.

Gambini responded, "There are commercial transport boats there. We need to get you on one of those boats. It will be dangerous to travel on the passenger ferry. The authorities may be looking for you there." The men agreed. All that was needed now was a way to get Raimondo onto one of the transports. The men continued their discussion as

Gambini's wife served them some food and wine. As she sat at the table with them, Raimondo noticed that she was blind in one eye, but he did not comment.

Gambini's wife had a brother who worked on a fishing trawler. The trawler would go out into the Mediterranean Sea four to six times a week to catch the bounty of fish that the sea held. Most of the fish would be delivered to the mainland through the port city of Reggio. The trawler captains would always have a reserve of extra workers for those times when the catches were heavy or someone got ill or injured. This would be the perfect opportunity to get Raimondo to the mainland. Gambini's brother-in-law would get Raimondo on the laborer's list. Then they would simply wait for the right day.

Gambini had Raimondo spend the next day with him in his home. He made arrangements for Raimondo's safe passage to Catania. On the evening before he left, Raimondo felt compelled to ask some questions of Gambini.

"You have been so kind and generous to me. I ask myself why?" Raimondo said to Gambini.

"Did you notice my wife is blind in her left eye?" Gambini replied.

" I noticed, but did not want to inquire," replied Raimondo.

"Three years ago, we were spending a holiday with her brother in Catania. My wife had taken my son along with her brother's wife and son for a stroll through the piazza. There was some trouble in the piazza with some local ruffians. The local authorities were called and soon arrived along with some *carabinieri* that were in Catania on a federal investigation. They quickly moved in to break up the melee." Tears began to well up in Gambini's eyes. "The *carabinieri* decided to open fire on the group of ruffians without any concern for the innocent bystanders who were in the piazza at the time. As the bodies began to fall, one of the *carabinieri* yelled out, *'Die Sicilian animals, die*!'" Gambini's head lowered, his chin now resting on his chest as he began to cry.

"My son... my innocent son... was hit in the chest. He died instantly." He wiped the tears from his eyes and let out a long sigh. Regaining his composure he finished the story. "My wife was struck by a pellet in her eye. She was blinded permanently. The *carabinieri* who did this is now a captain. The officials in Rome don't give a shit about Sicily. They treat us like bastard sons. They reward those who kill us like dogs in the street. Raimondo, this captain, his name is Morrisso. He is the man who is searching for you. So now you know why I am so willing to help. One day I will kill this son of a whore with my own hands."

"I am so sorry for your loss and your pain but very grateful for your assistance. I hope to someday be able to repay this debt to you," replied Raimondo.

SIX

Raimondo made his way to Catania with the assistance of Gambini's relatives. When he arrived in Catania, he was a guest of Gambini's brother-in-law. It was now a day-to-day wait. Gambini's brother-in-law had taken care of all the details of getting Raimondo placed on the standby laborer list. While he waited to be called, Raimondo was careful not to go out in public where he might be recognized.

He spent the day thinking about his brothers and his nephews and nieces and asked himself would he ever be able to return to Agrigento. For some time while in Agrigento, he had been noticing a beautiful girl who lived only a few streets away. She had long brown hair and pretty, bright smile. He was planning on approaching her father to ask for permission to court his daughter. In Sicily one always obtains permission before courting a young lady. Courtships are always short and always lead to marriage. There was no dating alone with a young girl. The so-called dates always take place with other family members of the girl present. This was done to preserve the virginity of the girl. Most of the marriages at this time were arranged marriages between families, with the young girls usually not having any say in the matter. It was always very advisable to have one of the elderly women of the village have a good look at the hips of the perspective bride, to be to certain that she would be able to bear children. He promised himself that if he could ever go back, he would marry this beautiful girl, but for now he did not even know her name.

On the third day of his stay the call for additional men on the trawler came. The catches were becoming heavier and the current crews on board the trawlers were having a difficult time hauling in the catches. More men were needed now because these heavy catches would not last forever. Raimondo prepared himself for the next day. He would assist on the trawler and then disappear into the crowd when the trawler docked in Reggio. Then it would be off to be reunited with his family, without the authorities ever knowing that any of them had left Sicily.

The trawler pulled out of port at 4 a.m. and headed out to the fertile waters off the Sicilian coast. It sailed through the Strait of Messina to an area where the catches had been abundant for the last few days. By noon the trawler was filled beyond capacity. It was time to take the day's catch to Reggio and offload. As the trawler headed back, the winds began to pickup. A sudden storm was sweeping across the sea. The winds were now blowing so strong that it pushed up huge waves over the bow of the trawler. It had become very dangerous to stay out in the high waves. All of the trawlers and many of the other commercial vessels that were in the area now rushed to get back to port. The commercial vessels would ride out the storm in Reggio and head back to sea when the storm had passed.

Raimondo had never been to sea before and the rocking motion of the trawler had begun to make him ill. He was nauseated and his head began to spin. He leaned over the side of the trawler and vomited extensively. He could barely stand up. One of the shipmates came over to him and helped him to an enclosed area of the trawler where he laid him down. This offered him some protection from the fierce storm raging outside. Raimondo had slipped on a pair of rubber boots over his shoes when he first arrived on the trawler. The shipmate was responsible for steering the vessel and had not put on a pair of rubber boots when the trawler had pulled out that morning. As the ship was anchored outside the port waiting its turn to enter the now busy port, the shipmate had to go out to check the bilge pump, which was emitting a loud a grinding noise. Raimondo was passed out on the control room floor of the vessel and the shipmate proceeded to remove his boots so he could wear them to go out onto the deck. He checked the pump and determined it was about to give out. The trawler had begun to take on some water and it was not clear where exactly from. He returned to the control room and summoned the captain.

There was not much time to lose. If the pump gave out completely the trawler was at risk of sinking. The port already had more vessels than it could handle. The captain decided to bypass Reggio and return to Catania with his load of fish. They would cross the strait the next day after the storm subsided and off load their catch. Suddenly there was smoke at the back of the ship where the pump was located. The pump had caught fire and was close to exploding. The crewmembers rushed to put out the fire. The captain then ordered the shipmate to steer the vessel into the port of Messina, which lay to the immediate west of the trawler. He was at this point convinced he would not make it to Catania, which was further south. The trawler, trailing a plume of thick black smoke, limped into Messina. The port authorities, noticing the smoke on the trawler, summoned the local police.

As soon as the trawler docked it was boarded by men offering to assist to put out the small fire, which was still burning in the pump room. The local police boarded, as well, and one entered the control room to question the captain. As he entered he noticed Raimondo still asleep on the floor.

"Is he injured?" asked the police officer.

"No, just very seasick," replied the captain. The captain went on to explain to the police officer the events that led up to the fire. He reassured the police officer that his crew was fine and that the only casualty they had suffered was a very seasick member of the crew.

"Why do you employ a man who gets seasick?" asked the police officer.

"He is new, a temporary worker we hired to help with the larger catches, this is his first trip," replied the captain, looking down at Raimondo.

Just then, as the police officer looked down, he noticed Raimondo's blood stained shoes. Suddenly he realized this could be the man that Morrisso could be looking for. He placed a handcuff around a pipe next to where Raimondo was sleeping and quietly slipped the other cuff around one of Raimondo's wrists. When Raimondo awoke, he found himself chained to the pipe. He knew at that time that his stop-and-go run was over. He continued to lie on the floor, staring up at the ceiling without uttering a word. A million thoughts raced through his head.

With some luck, Morrisso now had his man. His search was over. Raimondo who had by now been handcuffed and shackled was taken off the trawler and transported to the local jail to await his appearance before the local magistrate.

SEVEN

Six months had passed since Raimondo was imprisoned in Messina. He was still awaiting trial on the charges against him. The *carabinieri* that had been dispatched to Sicily to help maintain order had been recalled to the mainland as the political situation in Europe began to change. Without the presence of many of these officials who were essential witnesses in so many cases, the judicial process came to a grinding halt.

The European mainland was a powder keg of activity as Adolf Hitler and his Nazi Party grew in power. Before long, Germany was becoming a threat to its neighbors. A few years earlier political instability in Italy gave rise to the Fascist Party. Prior to the Fascist rise to power, the mainland politicians had a tendency to ignore the Sicilians and more or less treated its island neighbor as a poor little sister. With the winds of war blowing, Sicily became an important pawn in the Italian chess game.

On the surface Sicily was well known for its production of agricultural products such as wheat, olives, figs and other fruits. Sicily was also one of the world's largest producers of sulfur. Sulfur was a necessity in the production of bombs and other munitions. It was now time for Rome to recognize the importance of its little sister and maintain its source of sulfur to fuel its war machine.

Sicily had been firmly in the grasp and control of the Mafia to such an extent that it had control of the government on the island. Benito Mussolini, who was the head of the Fascist party, had seized control of the Italian government and became the new dictator. Recognizing the importance of its island neighbor to the south, he arranged for a trip to Sicily. There, he would assure the Sicilians, who were always on the outside, politically, that they would have a voice in his government.

Upon his arrival and accompanied by his bodyguards, he was greeted by the controlling Mafia don. The don told Mussolini that he did not need his bodyguards while he was in Sicily and that he would be under his protection. This infuriated Mussolini. He regarded the don's statement as one of contempt for his own government. He took it to mean that the don did not recognize the government in Rome and that the Sicilians had their own form of government. Mussolini began a campaign to crack down on the Mafia that lasted for several years.

While many of the mafia bosses were imprisoned, many others were fleeing the island and heading to America. The mafia had gone into hiding as its activities had been severely hampered by the crackdown. Still, the under bosses, in the absence of their leaders who fled or were imprisoned, managed whatever activity remained. Several of the bosses who fled now tried to maintain control from the other side of the Atlantic through the under bosses.

A new magistrate had been appointed in Messina after it was discovered that the magistrate's office had been sympathetic towards the mafia. The new magistrate was under orders from the provincial authorities to prosecute all mafia-related cases to the fullest extent. This was the opportune time for many of the people whose lives had been adversely affected by the mafia to cooperate with the authorities. The fear factor that so many Mafiosi had used to control the general population was now beginning to wane.

Aldo Pugliese had heard through some acquaintances in the magistrate's office that Raimondo's case was going to be heard in just a few weeks. He visited Raimondo in prison to discuss a plan, which he had devised. As he sat across from him at the table in the visiting area, he began to whisper to him the plan he had devised. "Do you remember the head *carabinieri* that pursued you? He was transferred to Milan. It seems that he was found to have dirty hands in his dealings here in Sicily." "You mean, Morrisso?" asked Raimondo.

"Yes," said Pugliese. He leaned forward in his chair and continued. "This could be your break. With the lack of witnesses it will be difficult to convict you. The two policemen that were shot have enlisted in the military and are not likely to return here to testify. The attorney I have hired feels we can make a case that you were set up by a Mafiosi sympathizer. With the strong sentiment against the Mafia, you may just stand a chance."

Tears began to fill Raimondo's eyes. "Aldo, you have been so good to my family. How will I ever repay you? I have spent so many days here, thinking about my family in Reggio and my sisters in America. I have wondered if I would ever see any of them again. I pray to God that this can happen. Thank you so much," said Raimondo as he embraced Pugliese.

"Don't thank me yet," said Pugliese. "The attorney will try to get your hearing date set soon. There is still much work to be done. With a little luck we can have success. Stay encouraged. I will come to visit again as soon as the date is set. Tomorrow the attorney will come to see you. Tell him everything. You can trust him. He will help you. I will get word to your family in Reggio. I pray that you will soon be reunited with your family."

He stood up, embraced Raimondo and headed for the door. When he reached the door he turned to Raimondo, smiled and with fists clinched together said, "Courage, always courage." He exited the small room accompanied by the prison guards.

Raimondo was led back to his cell by a prison guard. As the door to his cell was slammed and locked behind him, he thought to himself how lucky he was to have a friend as good as Pugliese. He smiled as he laid himself on his bunk. He kept hearing the words spoken to him by Pugliese. *"Courage, always courage."*

EIGHT

Within a matter of weeks the attorney who Pugliese had retained to represent Raimondo, had petitioned the magistrate to hear Raimondo's case. After reviewing the few documents that were available to him, the magistrate decided there was no longer any need to hold Raimondo in prison. The attorney had done his job. Raimondo was a free man.

Pugliese sent a carriage to pick up Raimondo from prison and bring him back to his home. To Raimondo's surprise, as he entered the home of Pugliese he was greeted by his brothers, nephews and nieces. Pugliese being confident that Raimondo would be freed had made arrangements to bring the family back to Messina for the joyful reunion. All the members of the Melina family cried as they embraced each other. Pugliese stood closely by, enjoying the wonderful moment. The Melina's would spend a few days in his home before moving on.

Pugliese, having had vast knowledge of the situation in Campobello, had taken advantage of the Andreo's misfortune by acquiring the olive groves and estate of Don Andreo at a very reasonable price. He was now ready to put the groves back into production. He offered Raimondo, Santo and Stefano employment at the groves and oil production facilities in Campobello. The brothers agreed, but only under one condition. They would have Pugliese hold a small amount of money from their pay until they could repay him for all the money he had spent in assisting them. Pugliese agreed and in a few days they would be on their way. Santo and Stefano would travel with Mama

Melina and the children to Campobello. Raimondo would spend some time in Agrigento to help Pugliese set up a warehouse and distribution facility there.

While in Agrigento, Raimondo inquired about the beautiful girl who had lived but a few streets away. Upon learning that she was unmarried and unpledged to anyone, he quickly set out to introduce himself to her father. Several days had passed when the young girl's father sent word to Raimondo that he would like to invite him to break bread with he and his family. Raimondo put on his Sunday best for his rendezvous.

After a brief courtship, Raimondo married Anna. Within three years she bore him three children, Enzo, Carina and Francesco. Life was going well for the Melinas. Steady work, modest but comfortable surroundings and a close family existence. Unfortunately, this was all about to come to an abrupt end.

The political situation in mainland Europe grew steadily worse. Hitler had rolled through Poland and was now preparing to conquer the rest of Europe. Normal commerce was disrupted and this was putting a strain on the business enterprises throughout Europe. Raimondo, his wife and children returned to Campobello just as the warehouse facility in Agrigento was closed due to a consolidation in the operations. Soon the entire business operation in Campobello came to a grinding halt. All of the workers were put out of work. The war made life difficult for the Sicilian people. Other than the increased production in the sulfur processing facilities, jobs now became very scarce. Once again, the mainland politicians chose to ignore the needs of the Sicilian people.

Raimondo had moved his family into a small house at the edge of town. The house essentially had four rooms. There were two bedrooms, a main living/cooking area and a separate area to keep two goats the family was raising. Food became scarcer as the war intensified. Meat, once again, became a scarcity as well as eggs and other basic food products. About the only food item that was in abundance were fave beans and the Melina family resorted to eating them three times a day in order to survive.

The skies over Campobello had become a popular place for dogfights between Allied and Axis fighter pilots. Many of the children would go out to the countryside after an aerial battle to loot the aircraft that had been shot down. Often times they would find food items, as well as the hardware items they would carry away. The realities of war also exposed them to the brutality of war. Burned and mutilated bodies were found on the downed aircraft. Many of the dead fighter pilots wore jewelry, which became easy pickings for the young looters. The Allied troops who had invaded Sicily in July of 1943 had established a base of operation nearby. It became a common practice for the young children to bring the dog tags of the dead pilots to the Allied troops in exchange for chocolate or other foods. Life, while not as comfortable as it had been, still went on. As is the case in nature—the fittest managed to survive.

The invasion of Sicily by Allied forces spelled the end of the Fascists reign in Italy. Within thirty-eight days the Allied troops had gained complete control of Sicily, as well as the world's major supply of sulfur. Soon afterwards the government in Rome fell. Mussolini was apprehended and killed. His body hung upside down in the piazza in Milan in total humiliation. The war in Sicily was over, but the hardships would continue.

After the war, those responsible for Mussolini's overthrow were rewarded by being given control of a large international oil conglomerate. This action created a new hierarchy in Italy and as their power base expanded both economically and politically, the corporate leaders of this new company posed a threat to the old orders in Sicily. Once again the new hierarchy was in conflict with the mafia.

With Mussolini and the fascists gone, the mafia was left to once again flourish. Once again the mafia bosses were exerting their influence and causing a stir in Rome. Eventually the mafia would eliminate the corporate leaders of the oil company by sabotaging an airplane carrying those top officials, sending them all to their deaths.

The allies were not too quick to help rebuild Italy, and Sicily certainly was a low priority. During the war it was discovered that the Melina family had claim to land, which contained a sulfur mine in Sicily. Raimondo had initiated an inquiry to obtain title to the land. At the same time some of the old vestiges of the Andreo clan had resurfaced.

Rumor had spread that they were planning to assassinate Raimondo. Fearing the worst and not wanting to leave his children fatherless, Raimondo fled with his family north to the Italian mainland. For now, his claim to the family-owned mine would have to wait. He would eventually emigrate to Belgium, where he found work as a coal miner. Anna bore him two more children, Stefano and Rita, while in Belgium. Brothers Stefano and Santo would eventually join them.

Being a coal miner was hard but steady work. There were also many risks involved. Many of the immigrants who arrived in Northern European countries after the war would find the dangers all too real as cave-ins and accidents were frequent. With little or no education, there were not many jobs for these immigrants to choose from. Despite the dangers, there was no shortage of immigrants to send down the shafts to mine the coal. The coalmine companies regularly paid a supplement to those who would work at the very deepest depths of the shafts.

There were also other obstacles to contend with. Learning a new language proved to be very difficult for many of the immigrants that arrived in northern Europe after the war. The coalmines were a true hodgepodge of various nationalities. The majority of the immigrants were comprised of men from Italy, Poland, Algeria and Morocco. Most of the ethnic groups kept to themselves and had little or no association with the other ethnic groups. This, often times, created friction between the groups and incidences of taunting were all too common.

Mine number forty-five, where Raimondo worked had a workforce comprised mainly of Italians and Poles. There were a handful of Algerian miners who worked alongside the Italians and Poles. For the most part, the workers coexisted peacefully. There was, however, one very large Algerian man who was constantly picking fights with the other workers. Because of his large size, the other men were reluctant to retaliate against this man. It was known that he packed a large curly knife in his workbag, which he used to intimidate the others. The Algerian had, for whatever reason, chosen to make Stefano a target of his hatred, taunting him and bumping him on every occasion.

On one particular night, Raimondo followed the Algerian and Stefano to the bottom level of the shaft. Once again, the Algerian taunted and pushed the other workers. He pushed Stefano so hard that he knocked him against the wall of the shaft, cutting his head. While the Algerian was preoccupied harassing the other workers, Raimondo removed the curly knife from his bag. He passed by the Algerian with the knife hidden under his coat. The Algerian decided that he would push Raimondo, as well, when he walked by him. Just as he went to push him, Raimondo pulled the knife and passed it cleanly through the Algerian man's midsection. He pulled the knife back through and out, disemboweling him. The other workers stared in disbelief. While they were shaken by what had happened, they were also relieved that the harassment had come to an end. They collaborated on a story that Raimondo had acted in self-defense after being attacked. Because many of the workers had reported the harassment on so many previous occasions to the mining officials, the police accepted the story the miners presented them with. Raimondo was never charged for killing him.

Raimondo's oldest son, Enzo, followed after his father as a coal miner. With seven mouths to feed, Enzo's earnings were also needed to sustain the family. Enzo married Louise at age twenty-one and the newlyweds moved in with his family. The small house that the coalmine company provided as housing became cramped and uncomfortable for the Melinas as Enzo and Louise produced two male children in a two-year period. Enzo secretly yearned for a better life, but jobs were limited for someone with little education. What he feared most, was being killed in a mining accident and leaving his young wife and children behind. He dreamed of a better life.

What Raimondo did not know was that Enzo was secretly writing to his Aunt Vincenza in America, who had filed the necessary sponsorship paperwork to bring Enzo and his young family to America. After several months, the INS had approved Enzo's application and he would soon be on his way to America with his family. While Raimondo did not want his son to leave, he accepted the fact that he was in pursuit of a better life. Enzo told his father that as soon as he made enough money, he would sponsor the remaining members of his family to come to America.

Leaving would not be easy. Enzo had made several close friends while in Belgium. He had learned the language and was well respected amongst his circle of friends, both Sicilians and non-Sicilians alike. Although still relatively young, he was often consulted by his older friends for advice on matters of importance. One of his closest friends, Nino San Marco, was deeply troubled when he learned that Enzo would soon be leaving. Enzo had helped Nino adjust to his new homeland when he had first arrived in Belgium. Nino was tall and lanky and had a full head of very curly hair. This made him an easy target to have fun poked at by the local kids. Enzo responded by giving a good ass beating to those perpetrators. It wasn't long before the name calling stopped. Nino never forgot what his friend did for him.

Enzo and Nino would swear an oath of allegiance to each other, to always remain friends and be ready to come to the other's aid if necessary. They wandered off into the wheat fields together and with the shaft of a blade of wheat cut their fingers and drew blood. They then dripped their blood onto a rock and mixed it with the wheat until it became one, thus symbolizing their unity and undying friendship.

Enzo would also have to deal with leaving his siblings behind. Especially difficult, would be parting with the two youngest. Stefano and Rita were born after their arrival in Belgium and little Stefano now only 4 years old was almost like a shadow to his big brother. Stefano also loved being around his nephews, Alex and Nunzio. Nonetheless, Enzo felt he had to pursue a better life. He was confident that in time he would be able to arrange for the rest of his family to join him in America. So off he went with his young wife and two infant children to a new world, which awaited him.

NINE

After spending five days on the open sea, Enzo could see the shoreline of America as he stood on the deck of the ocean liner. As the *S.S. Queen Mary* drew closer to the coast, he could see the image of the Statue of Liberty appear on the horizon. The Grande Dame was greeting him as she had greeted millions of others who had made their way to the shores of America. He quickly made his way back to his cabin to inform Louise that New York was within view.

Louise had spent much of the journey ill in her cabin and was not at all anxious to stand on deck where the rolling action of the waves would make her sicker.

"Take your sons with you and show them America. Tell them we came here to give them a better life. I'll wait for you here," she said.

Enzo quickly put warm clothes on his two sons and took them onto the deck into the cold January air. "Look my sons: America. This is where you'll grow big and strong and be successful," he said to his two young sons. It was not long before the cold air sent Enzo and his sons back to the warmth of their cabin.

After docking at the New York harbor, Enzo, pulling behind him a green handmade trunk, made his way to the taxi stand outside the harbor facility. Following closely behind, with two infants in her arms was a debilitated Louise. As they stood in the taxi line, Louise became ill. Handing her two sons to Enzo, she began to vomit violently and went crashing to the pavement as she passed out. One of the cab drivers quickly came over to assist.

"Let me help you," he said to Enzo.

"No speak English," Enzo replied in his broken English.

"*Sei Italiano*?" asked the cab driver.

"*Siciliano*," replied Enzo.

They began to converse in Italian as the cab driver helped Louise into his cab and loaded the green trunk into the trunk of the cab.

"When we get to the train station, I'll help you get your tickets so you will be ready to board your train. You just stay with your wife and children and keep an eye on that trunk of yours," the driver said to Enzo as they drove towards the train station.

"Every thing I have in life is with me, my wife, my sons and whatever is in the trunk," replied Enzo.

The driver stayed with Enzo and his young family until it was time to board. After helping them board the train and being certain that they were all well situated, he returned to his cab to continue his shift.

Nine hours later the train rolled into the station in Buffalo. His aunt Vincenza and Uncle Ignazio, whom he referred to as Pina and Pino, greeted Enzo. After a short cab ride, they arrived at his aunt's house. Louise, still ill from the voyage, went directly to bed. Enzo tended to his two young sons as he dined with his aunt and uncle. They discussed a job search strategy for Enzo. Enzo understood from the dinner conversation that while his aunt did sponsor him to come to America, there were no long-term plans to allow Enzo and his family to stay with his aunt and uncle any longer than absolutely necessary. Enzo was set to search for work the very next day.

After a restful night sleep, Enzo accompanied by Pina set out the very next morning into the neighborhood to look for work. They visited all of the business establishments in the immediate neighborhood. Many of the shopkeepers and business owners in the neighborhood were of Italian descent or were immigrants themselves. Several of them had agreed to keep Enzo in mind, in case any job openings became available. For now, there were no job openings. One of the shopkeepers suggested that Enzo visit a new local restaurant outside of the immediate neighborhood that was set to open in about three days.

The next day Enzo accompanied once again by his Pina, presented himself at the restaurant to apply for a job. Since he did not speak English, Aunt Pina did the talking for him. The restaurant owner agreed to hire Enzo to work in the kitchen, washing dishes and cleaning. What Enzo did not realize was that, although Pina and Pino had been in the country for many years, they still had not mastered the English language very well. There was not much need to when most of your life was centered in a neighborhood where everyone, including all the business establishments, spoke Italian. As a result of this language barrier, the agreed upon wage was considerably less than other business establishments were willing to pay for unskilled labor. The next day Enzo reported for work, eager to begin his new life in America.

After about thirty days, Enzo had made the acquaintances of several other immigrants from the region of Sicily where his family had lived. He soon discovered that based on their employment status, he was terribly underpaid and overworked. Many of them had after several months of arriving in America, been lucky enough to secure jobs with firms in the construction industry, either as apprentices or as general laborers. He began to inquire as to how to go about landing one of those jobs for himself. He approached his employer through an interpreter and inquired about a raise in his hourly wage. His employer responded by telling him that he should be happy that he was kind enough to give him and the rest of his grease ball buddies a job and he could leave if he wanted to. Enzo, while deeply offended at his employer's remarks, chose to stay. He did, after all, have a family to feed.

Since the dishwashers and cleaners changed clothing before and after their shifts, they carried a duffle bag to hold their clothing and shoes. Enzo decided he would earn his fair wage by helping himself to some food items from the kitchen, which he would hide in his duffle bag and sneak out of the restaurant after his shift. Meats, cheeses and baked goods found their way into Louise's kitchen several times a week. Whenever she inquired as to the cost, Enzo would simply say they were getting old and the restaurant owner did not want them to go to waste, so he allowed the employees to take them home.

Two months had passed and Enzo, Louise and their children moved into the downstairs flat next door to Pina and Pino's. The flat was cold and cramped but it was a start for Enzo and his young family. Since Pino owned the property, he gave Enzo a break on the rent each month. Enzo had set aside some money and was able to buy a bed for he and Louise. Their infant children slept in cribs donated by some friends. Still, Enzo prayed that he would soon be called to work in the construction industry where he could earn a very respectable living. Later that spring, his break came. The construction boom was in full swing and contractors were calling the laborers union every day for additional laborers. While at the restaurant, he received a visit from one of his *paesans* who told him to go to the union office to fill out his papers and he would be placed on a job site the next day. Enzo decided to finish his shift and before leaving helped himself to a complete set of silverware, which he very promptly packed in his duffle bag. He received some curious looks from the other bus riders that night as his bag clanged with every stop.

The next morning, Enzo took the bus to the union hall and filled out the necessary paperwork to begin work. He was asked to report to a job site the very next day. He was assigned to the Tergen Construction Company. As luck would have it, his *paesan* Phil, a tile mason by trade, was working the same job site. Enzo not only had a good paying job, he also had a ride to and from the job site. Knowing that he would still be at that site after the tile masons moved on, Enzo took his drivers test and received his driver's license. Within a month he would buy his very first car. He would now have his own ride to work. Life was moving along in the right direction for Enzo and his family.

Several years passed and Enzo continued to work steadily. He attended many of the monthly union meetings with several of his *paesans* and it was then that he realized that the local mafia controlled the union. This did not bother Enzo and his *paesans* in the least, as they were happy to have fellow Sicilians and Italians in control. They received excellent wages and top-notch benefits. While the work was extremely hard, it was very rewarding and the union members were very grateful to their officers for the way they were taken care of. For this reason, they did not care what activity the union officials were engaged in outside of the union.

Pina had come to America with several of her sisters many years earlier. Her sister, Angela, was widowed at an early age and had a son named Charlie. She had disowned Charlie late in his teen years. Charlie had a police record as long as a city block. He had been arrested for everything from narcotics possession to gambling to assault and battery. He was also believed to associate with some of the mobsters from the local labor union.

Charlie was always on the lookout for new recruits to help him with his criminal activities. He especially liked to prey on newly landed immigrants who were struggling financially.

One day while he was returning home from work, Charlie approached Enzo. "Hey *paesan*! I'm your cousin, Charlie. I came by to introduce myself," Charlie said striking up a conversation with Enzo. During the course of the conversation Charlie had convinced Enzo to help him with some furniture moving jobs on Saturday.

Unbeknownst to Enzo at the time, this was to be a burglary. That evening while visiting Pina and Pino, Enzo mentioned that he was going to help Charlie with a moving job over the weekend. After getting the full story of Charlie's life from his aunt and uncle, Enzo thought better of helping Charlie. That Saturday, Enzo did not show up at the appointed time, as previously planned.

Pina had yet another sister, named Concetta, who had married a successful farm owner and moved to Collins, an agricultural community outside of Buffalo. Concetta had two sons who were the same age as Enzo. Enzo had grown close to them and he enjoyed visiting them on weekends. It seemed to Enzo that the country air was cleaner and more relaxing than where he lived in the city and he loved the quiet surroundings there.

One particular Sunday, after having finished his visit with his cousins, Enzo and his family headed home. He pulled off to the side of the road to gather some tomatoes from one of the fields at his uncle's farm. Louise and his two young sons joined him. As Enzo walked away from his family further into the field, he heard a loud blast off to his right. Instantaneously a bullet struck the ground not far from where he stood. He quickly shouted to Louise to get the children back to the car. Once again a shot rang out and once again a bullet struck the ground nearby. Enzo looked across the road to another field and saw a man who had a striking resemblance to Charlie getting into a car and driving away. He joined his family in the car and drove directly home.

Enzo's biggest worry now was not for his safety, but for that of his family. He realized that Charlie was retaliating for his being a no show at the burglary and began to understand just how violent and dangerous Charlie was. He swore he would kill Charlie with his own hands if he tried to harm his family. His worries would soon be over. The next day, as Louise walked her children to school, she witnessed Charlie beating a man to death with a chain at a corner gas station. She quickly whisked her children across the street and continued her walk to school. When she arrived home, she learned that Charlie had been arrested for murder. Knowing that Charlie would be in prison for many years to come was a great relief to Enzo.

Up to this point in time, Enzo's experience in America had been a pleasant one. He had gained the respect of his co-workers and was well liked by his employers. He had become a well skilled, highly productive cement finisher. His employers often asked him to work overtime and on weekends, much to his liking. He used the extra earnings to pay for the tuition at a private Catholic school for his sons and was saving the rest for a down payment on a home. Despite the fact that he was treated so well by his employers, he also dreamed of one day owning his own construction company.

The mob-controlled laborer's union was instrumental in keeping out-of-state companies from ever successfully bidding on local construction projects. This protected the local construction companies and assured the union of keeping the majority of their members gainfully employed and paying their dues. In return for this protection, the union required all local construction companies to employ only card-carrying union members. Each employer designated an on the job union member or union steward to submit a roster of workers who had been on the job site each week. This report was sent directly to the union office every Friday at the end of the workday. The list was very carefully checked by the union' business office to assure that every worker was a dues paying union member. It was also not uncommon for union business officials to visit the job sites and perform routine audits. This practice kept everyone honest. The penalty for non-compliance was severe. Companies that did not comply had a difficult time getting laborers from the union labor pool or were sent the least reliable men. Any worker on the job who refused to join the union was threatened and harassed and in some cases beaten by mob-appointed enforcers.

Because of his reliability, Enzo was assigned the responsibility of union steward for his employer. Every Friday, Enzo would submit his report to the union office. He was paid a small fee, weekly, direct from the union for this task and was required to attend monthly meetings on union matters. His promptness in submitting his reports and his one hundred percent attendance at the monthly meetings had begun to get him noticed by union officials. He would often stay after the meetings to fraternize with the other stewards and union officials. He seemed to take a keen interest in the overall operation of the union and the benefits its members were deriving. He understood that a strong union meant better wages and benefits for its members. In a few short years, Enzo had gone from being an overworked, underpaid dishwasher to a well-paid cement finisher and a union steward in one of the most powerful labor unions in America.

Using the skills he had gained as a cement finisher, Enzo began to do small concrete side jobs on his own on weekends. Since he was allowed to take his employers truck home after work hours, he did not have to invest in a work truck. To his benefit, the truck was also loaded with all the tools he needed to do his work. Soon, he would be doing side work after his regular work hours on weekdays, as well. With his side jobs Enzo raked in enormously large profits. Since he was using his employer's equipment, he had no investment in tools or machinery. He had also managed to bribe the concrete truck drivers to deliver excess concrete to his side jobs. Enzo's side jobs were pure profit. Within a few months his business had grown to the point where he took on a partner and had to hire extra workers to keep up with the demand for his services. It was out of this demand that he finally started his own company, the Melina Concrete Construction Company. Since he had virtually no overhead, he was able to be more competitive than any other concrete paving company in the area. His services were in such high demand that he had to turn away potential jobs. Enzo had also become very bold throughout this period of time. He had magnetic signs with his company name and logo made to place over the painted "Tergen Construction" company name on his employer's equipment. It was full speed ahead for Enzo in fulfilling his dream of owning his own company. His business venture and his status amongst his piers was growing. Enzo soon discovered that was not all that was growing. Louise was pregnant and expecting their third child.

TEN

Despite her feelings of loneliness, Louise was happy to once again be carrying a child. Her two sons were quickly growing and were less dependent on her with each passing day. It seemed as though Enzo was never home anymore. After finishing his daily duties with Tergen Construction, Enzo headed directly to his own company's job sites to assist his hired crew. During the concrete pour season, which lasted from April through November, it was not uncommon for Enzo to return home after midnight. This left Louise with the load of the household responsibilities and tending to the boys.

Enzo became a member of the Campobello Social Organization, which was made up of immigrant men from his old country village of Campobello. The organization's main function was to organize social events for its members and assist newly landed immigrants in settling into their new environment. On the quiet side, there were also organized weekend card games held in the basement of a local barbershop owned by one of its members. The card games attracted dozens of players and, occasionally, some labor union officials. Here, Enzo had the opportunity to socialize with the more elite of the *paesans* and exchange business ideas.

Despite the fact that Enzo was busy with his work schedule, he always managed to include his sons, Nunzio and Alex, in his weekend activities. The boys especially liked going to the wrestling matches with their father and stopping at the local "beef on weck" joint for a roast beef sandwich afterwards. Often times he would take them to his job sites where they would play with their army trucks in the sand. At the same time, Louise was feeling neglected and lonely. With none of her own family nearby and few friends, Louise grew increasingly isolated and depressed. After nine long and lonely months, Louise gave birth to a beautiful baby girl, which they named Catalina.

Barely six months had passed after the birth of Catalina when Louise had begun to exhibit signs of severe depression. With Enzo refusing to address her depression, she chose what she felt was the only course available to her. One night while Enzo was working late Louise attempted to take her own life by swallowing a bottle of sleeping pills. She was found unconscious by Nunzio and Alex, who called Pina and Pino when their mother was unresponsive. She managed to survive and was hospitalized for several weeks.

Louise returned home, experiencing the same feelings she felt prior to her suicide attempt. It appeared that Enzo began to distance himself from Louise. Their relationship had seemed to evolve into more of a master-servant relationship than one of husband and wife. Enzo with all of the money and power was the dominant person and called all the shots. At times he belittled Louise and on occasion pulled her hair or struck her. It was almost as if their lives were being played out in old time Sicily.

One day after he had returned home from work, Louise approached Enzo with a request. "I want to go to Belgium for a vacation to visit my mother. I will take Catalina with me. Pina and Pino can look after the boys while I am gone."

Enzo threw his hands in the air, shrugged his shoulders and replied. "Go back to Belgium to visit your mother; leave my sons and me here, what the hell is the matter with you? These are your kids and your responsibility. You are not going anywhere. You cannot go!"

Louise began to cry, " I feel like a slave here, like I have no purpose in life but to wait on you and the children. I have no family or friends here. I am alone."

Enz,o turning red in the face, now approached his wife. "You damn bitch, what better purpose is there in life but to take care of those you love. We are your family. You have friends!" Enzo shouted back.

"No, Enzo, they are your friends!" she replied.

Enzo shouted louder. "Shut up! You should be thankful for what you have. What purpose in life do I have, huh? To take care of my family, work hard, provide you with nice things. What more do you want, you whore?"

Louise, now crying harder, replied, "Whore! Whore! I am no whore. I am a good and faithful woman." Louise was now curled into a ball in the corner of the room as Enzo approached her with a raised and clenched fist. Before he could strike her, a hand, seemingly out of nowhere, grabbed his arm and pulled him away. It was his Aunt Pina.

"Louise, take Catalina and go next door. Ignazio, take the boys outside. Enzo, you go in the kitchen and pour yourself some wine, we should talk," his aunt, taking charge, addressed those in the room.

As they all left the room, Enzo went to the kitchen poured himself a glass of wine and sat down at the table. Pina now entered the room. "Enzo, what are you doing?" she asked. "All this screaming and yelling, it is not good for your children. And your wife, she cries all the time, she is not happy. Do you want to loose her and your children? If something happens to her what are you going to do?" she asked Enzo.

Enzo replied in a harsh tone, "Son of a bitch, she is never happy!"

Pina interrupted him, "Stop! Stop now. You do not realize what you are doing here. I hear both of you all the time. Enough with all this fighting. She cries to me in the daytime when you are not here. Enzo, she is a woman, your wife, not a slave. This is not the Sicily of your grandfather. This is America!" Pina continued. "Sometimes a woman needs something different than a man. I left my mother and father behind also. I know what the pain is that she is feeling. To deny her is wrong."

Enzo sipped from his wine glass, not daring to interrupt. Putting her arm around him, she said to him, "You have money now. You should buy your own house. Let her pick new furniture. It will make her feel useful. I do not want to see you go away from us here, but it is time. Then you should allow her mother to come and visit. Tell her you will pay for half the trip. You go pick her up in New York."

Enzo replied. " I want to build a new house outside the city. She does not want to go there. What am I to do?"

Pina answered him. "To go out of the city puts her more out of contact with everything and everyone. Look for a house in the city. You can go fancy later. And one more thing, teach her how to drive." Enzo raised his eyebrows. Pointing her finger at him she sternly said to him, "Be yourself, not your father."

Enzo stood up and smiled. Nodding his head in the affirmative he said to her, "Okay, okay, I'll take care of it."

"One day you will realize that I was right," she said to him. "You will be happy we had this discussion. I'm making some pasta with broccoli. Come on next door and join us. Later you can make things right with her."

The entire family sat down to a pasta dinner together. It was a very quiet affair with only a few words exchanged between Enzo and his wife. After dinner Enzo, Louise, and the children headed back to their flat. Enzo put the boys to bed and went back to his bedroom. Louise had already put Catalina in her crib and was in bed when Enzo entered the room.

"Are you sleeping?" Enzo asked Louise. "I want to talk to you."

"You said enough earlier," she said to him.

"Do you want to hear what I have to say?" he asked.

"Say what you have to say," she said. "I'm tired and want to go to sleep."

"This weekend we will go look for a house. In the city," he said. " Then you can pick out some new furniture."

Louise sat up in bed. "You mean that?" she asked. "You really mean that?"

"Are you happy now?" Enzo asked.

"Yes, I'm happy," she responded.

"Good, then turn off the lights and come here," he said to her. She turned off the lights and slid close to him in the bed. The next morning, before leaving for work, he told her to write her mother and tell her she could visit her in the states. Louise was thrilled at the news. She began to write her letter immediately.

Within two months Enzo had moved his family to a large two story house on the upper west side. Louise had very tastefully decorated their new home. The boys shared a bedroom while Catalina occupied the third bedroom. Louise was very proud of her new surroundings. To make matters even better, Enzo had taught Louise how to drive and bought her a used car. Louise's mother came to visit shortly thereafter. After a brief visit, her mother returned to Belgium. For now at least she was content. Her depression seemed to go away.

While their relationship did not improve on an emotional level, Louise was somewhat fulfilled by the financial resources that were available to her. She took advantage of the availability of money to her to purchase a rather extensive new wardrobe for herself. After several years of sacrificing her own needs for those of her boys, it was now time to take care of herself. She managed to fill her days taking care of her children and socializing with her neighbors. She fulfilled her obligation to her husband by caring for his children and maintaining their home. While she despised having to do so, she kept Enzo content in the bedroom, as well.

The years passed and their children grew. Enzo and Louise grew further apart emotionally, but managed to keep a happy face on their marriage. As the children grew older they relied on Louise to get them to most of their extra-curricular activities. She was also very active in keeping up with their progress in school, meeting with their teachers and keeping them on course. She was influential in steering them to practice their Catholic faith, accompanying them to church every Sunday and Holy Day of Obligation. She encouraged them to pray and have faith in God to deliver all their needs. With her encouragement Alex and Nunzio served as altar boys in their local parish. Enzo managed to attend church on Easter Sunday every year and as needed for funerals.

Because of her gentleness and caring spirit, the children felt comfortable turning to their mother for advice. They would often take the time to discuss important matters in their lives with her, knowing that she was always willing to listen. Enzo was different. He seemed to have a harsher approach to life in general. When he dispensed advise it was usually harsh and critical. He had a tremendous distrust of others. His methods of discipline always involved corporal punishment and his children feared his heavy hand. While he did truly love them, he did not possess the gentler side of parenting skills necessary to be a gentle disciplinarian. He had never been exposed to them in his own childhood. There was no doubt his children loved him, but they feared him even more.

While Enzo and Louise had two differing styles of childrearing, the combination worked well for their children. The children learned gentleness and caring from Louise and drive and ambition from Enzo. One thing that was evident in the children was the fact that they were very close to each other. Alex and Nunzio were so close in age that they were rarely seen apart. Catalina being the baby sister of the clan was always under the watchful eye of her older brothers. As they grew older the bond between them grew tighter, even as the bond between their parents diminished. While they realized this fact they never questioned it; it was not something that was discussed in a Sicilian household.

As the years went on, Enzo was able to sponsor his own mother, father, and brothers, Francesco and Stefano, to reside in the United States. Obtaining immigrant status for Raimondo was a very difficult task because of the legal issues in his past. Enzo received help from some of his union contacts to help in the process. Approval finally came after several years of being apart and Enzo was elated. He would now have his family together in the United States. He rented out the upstairs flat of his house to them so they would always be close by. Enzo was now spending most of his free time visiting with his parents and less time paying attention to Louise.

It became more apparent as time went on that there was no love between Enzo and Louise. Their being together was simply a matter of convenience. Louise's attempts at becoming a more independent woman were met with stiff resistance from Enzo. This further deteriorated their relationship. The verbal and physical abuse between them grew worse as time went on and now it was not Pina who would come over to intervene, but Enzo's parents. There was nothing left of the relationship. Louise had decided she would wait until her children were finished with college before she would end their marriage.

ELEVEN

Enzo had clearly established himself in the area construction industry. After only a few short years he had transformed Melina Concrete Construction Company into a fast-growing development company. Melina Development Corporation was becoming a major player in the real estate and development arena. Although he had parted ways with Tergen Construction, Enzo often times partnered with his past employer on construction projects. His financial independence allowed him to finance his own company, without the help of a partner. With Nunzio having completed college and having earned his degree in engineering, it was not long before he joined Enzo in the business. Stefano went to work for Enzo, as well, while Alex continued his studies in pre-med.

Enzo's money and power base were growing in other ways, as well. Ever since his cousin, Charlie, had gone to jail on a murder charge, much of his illicit business activity had become disorganized and was crumbling. Because Charlie had become so openly violent he had lost the police protection needed to keep his operations going. The police captains and patrolmen received a hefty payment to ignore silent operations, such as bookmaking and prostitution. It was, however, difficult to ignore headline-grabbing events, such as beatings and murder.

Enzo had heard that the bookmaking operation raked in several thousand dollars a week. He arranged a meeting with the former principals of the operation. He offered to bankroll the operation in return for a fifty percent cut of the take. This was significantly less than Charlie would take from the operation and the former principals jumped at the opportunity to get back in the business. Enzo would also use his influence with the local police captains, getting them to look the other way when it came to his other business dealings.

One of the former principals of the bookmaking operation was Raul Acosta, a Cuban whose family fled the island nation prior to Castro's takeover. Raul's family had a large stake in a pipe manufacturing operation in Cuba and was able to transfer most of the assets to the United States prior to the communist takeover. Raul had hooked up with Charlie mostly out of boredom and not necessity. He was the mastermind who put together the entire bookmaking and gambling operation for Charlie. He was good at what he did and knew it, but for some unknown reason, allowed Charlie to screw him out of earnings he was rightfully due. Raul jumped at the opportunity to work for Enzo and within 30 days had the old operation up and running once again. What he could not arrange was the police protection needed to maintain his operation. That he left up to Enzo.

Enzo was on a first-name basis with many of the police captains throughout the city and was friends with the chief of police. His company had been awarded a significant contract to remodel several of the precinct houses throughout the city. During the course of the work, he had become friendly with several of the captains and lieutenants and sent crews to their homes to put in new concrete steps or sidewalks. All the work at their homes was done free of charge in order to gain favors from the police. The strategy worked. Enzo had gained their trust and friendship. Enzo approached several of them and asked them to look the other way and ignore his bookmaking operation. He offered to pay them a small fee in return for their cooperation. They not only agreed to cooperate but also became steady customers. With the police in their back pocket, Raul was able to operate without the fear of legal complications.

Enzo also inquired about some of Charlie's other operations, but viewed them as risky business ventures. What he was really concerned with was some of the people that ran the other operations for Charlie. Enzo viewed them as too high profile, people who wanted to be in the limelight no matter what it took. Many of them often bragged about what they did for a living, mostly done to come off as being tough and to impress the women.

Enzo, on the other hand, chose to remain very low profile. He did not need to impress anyone; he already had a lot of money from his development company. He believed that the key to longevity in illegal operations was to stay out of the limelight. Conduct your business peacefully, collect your money and stay quiet. Above all, surround yourself with people who share the same philosophy.

He decided to go it on his own with some of the other operations, cutting out the button men who were involved in running them. This did not sit well with many of them and they immediately turned to Tony Riccio, the ranking business manager at the local laborer's union. Tony had financed several of Charlie's illicit operations in the past and was given a cut of the take in return for his investment. Tony had been so busy with negotiating new labor contracts for the last year that he had ignored what was happening on the streets. Having learned that someone else had stepped in and taken charge, he now wanted his fair share. He sent his emissary to contact Enzo's people to make his request.

Enzo had hired a sharp and business-savvy bricklayer named Al Ganado to help manage the everyday business of his development company. The two had met at Tergen Construction and had become close friends. Al had made quite a bit of money developing a pre-fabricated brick board for interior use. Most of the local contractors were using his product in their remodel jobs, as it was a very fashionable item at the time. Al had endured the tragedy of loosing his son in a car accident and had taken a year off from the construction business to spend time with his wife and daughters. He did not need to work as his brick board sales brought in substantial income. Enzo approached him and offered him the job of Director of Construction Operations. Enzo told him that when he was ready, the job was his. After a few months of pondering, Al accepted and went to work for Enzo. Al was also, to a small extent, involved in some of Enzo's other activities but these were mostly confined to obtaining looted construction equipment and supplies for use in the construction operations.

Tony Riccio's emissary made his initial contact with Al. Al not being overly involved in Enzo's other operations put off arranging a meeting until he could talk with Enzo. Al caught up with Enzo later on that day at a construction site. "Hey boss, let's go get a cup of coffee," he said to Enzo.

Enzo replied, "We got fresh coffee in the office, we get some from there."

"Okay," said Al, "but let's walk so we can talk in private."

The two men poured their coffee and headed outside for a stroll. "One of Riccio's guys called me today, wants to have a meeting about some payments that are due to him. I didn't know what to say so I told him I had to check my schedule. He said, 'What the fuck you mean check your schedule?' Enzo, I did not know what else to say! I hope this does not cause you any trouble."

Enzo replied, "Al, no worry about it. We take care of it."

"If you don't mind my asking, what's it about?" asked Al.

"I guess he thinks I should pay him some money like Charlie did," Enzo said.

"There is one difference. I use my money and not his, so why I should pay him?"

"Sounds tricky," said Al.

"I send Nunzio and Stefano to talk to this *testa dura* (hard head)," said Enzo.

Enzo had Al call to set up the meeting so that Tony would think it was Al they would be dealing with. While Al was a good businessman he was not capable of dealing with powerful men in tricky situations. Al set the meeting place at a local restaurant. Enzo had to send a message that he was not afraid of Tony.

Enzo sent Nunzio and Stefano to meet with Tony's emissary. The emissary who was expecting Al was surprised to see Nunzio and Stefano arrive. The three men sat down at a table together as Tony's emissary began to speak

Stefano stood up and told him to shut up and listen. Feeling outnumbered and vulnerable, he did just that. Nunzio then began to speak. "My father respects the fact that Tony was assisting with these operations in the past. This is a new ball game now. Tony's money is not involved here and neither are any of his people."

Nunzio stood up and walked around the table where they were seated.

"Because my father is a reasonable person we offer this. We will pay Tony an amount equal to what he was getting, based on what the take was at the time Charlie's operation went down. No pay on any new ventures. Right now that includes the bookie operations and that's all. That's our offer."

Stefano now slid a manila envelope stuffed with thousands of dollars towards the emissary. "This shows that we are fair people," Stefano said.

The emissary looked inside. "And what if that is not good enough?" he asked. Stefano and Nunzio both shrugged their shoulders as they left the room.

Nunzio and Stefano began to converse as they got into their vehicle. "What did you think Unc?" asked Nunzio.

"I think the bastard was scared," replied Stefano. " He was expecting skinny little Al and he got us two crazies instead."

"I thought I heard him pissing in his pants," Nunzio replied, laughing.

"I hope they don't like the deal, then we got an excuse to go out and kick some ass," said Stefano.

"Slow down Unc, we gotta stay low profile, remember," Nunzio replied.

"If we are gonna be gangsters we gotta break some knees," Stefano said.

Nunzio replied, "Gangsters we are not, we are businessmen, remember."

"Yeah, with a big stick," replied Stefano. "Let's go home and let your father know what happened."

They soon arrived at Enzo's house. Both men entered the door, Nunzio greeted his mother with a kiss and asked, "Where's Pops?"

"He's on the patio," she replied. Nunzio and Stefano headed out to the patio.

"Hey Joffa, you back already?" asked Enzo who was lying in his lounger. "How did it go?"

"I think he was surprised to see me and Nunz," Stefano replied. "He's only the messenger."

They continued to fill Enzo in on the details of the meeting.

"What do we do if they say no?" asked Nunzio.

Enzo stood up and lit a cigar. "We worry about that when we get to it. Good work guys, you did good," he said. " He can hurt me a little bit with job bids, he can make things difficult for us there. We could miss out on some big jobs but he can't stop it all. If we let him think we're scared he'll run over us."

Enzo sat down at the table. "Tony's biggest problem is the damn drug business he is in." Now that the *tootsoons* and *Potoricanos* are in it, he's loosing some of his sources. The suppliers sell to those guys because they pay them more money for the drugs." Enzo took a big puff of his cigar as Stefano and Nunzio listened attentively. "He's getting squeezed," Enzo said. "I don't think he can fight too many battles at once, and right now the *tootsoons* and spics are his bigger problem. If it wasn't, he would have had someone taking over Charlie's old thing by now."

"I hope you're right," said Nunzio.

"Fuck him, let's take him out now and not worry about it," said Stefano. "If he is vulnerable now we should take advantage."

"Not good thinking," replied Enzo. "We got the local police and judges in our pocket now, if we want to get bigger we are gonna need some of Tony's allies later." Enzo now gestured towards Stefano and said to him, "Slow down, don't be so quick to pull the trigger. What we offered Tony was better than he had last month. We just wait."

As Stefano, Enzo and Nunzio headed back into the house they heard Alex coming in the front door and greeting his mother with a hug. "*Mamina,* "he said to her. "Hey Nunz, hey Uncle," he said to the others. "You guys leaving?"

Nunzio replied, "We knew you were coming," as he laughed.

"Hey Pops, tell my big brother to stop giving his little brother shit," Alex said to Enzo as he went over and hugged his brother.

"We just came over to fill Dad in on our meeting with Tony Riccio's people," Nunzio said to Alex.

"I told you guys before, leave him out of this shit," Enzo replied.

"Hey Pops, stop treating me like a pussy. You think I don't know what goes on around here?" Alex said to his father.

"You *fogetabout* this and study to be a doctor, that's why I pay for your school," Enzo shouted back.

Stefano cupped his hands over his mouth and said, "Calling Doctor Melina, calling Doctor Melina, you are wanted at the Your Host Restaurant for coffee."

Stefano and Nunzio left and were soon followed by Alex, where they rendezvoused at the restaurant to fill Alex in on the day's happenings.

Enzo, while worried what Tony's next move would be, was content to wait it out, hoping that Tony would not risk a war over Enzo pushing his way into the business. Deep down inside, Enzo knew that at this point in time he did not have the muscle to go against Tony. He was gambling that Tony, not really knowing how much muscle Enzo had or did not have, would not want to risk finding out.

When Tony got word from his emissary of what had happened at the meeting he was furious. "Who the hell are these people? Where did they come from all of a sudden?" he asked out loud.

The emissary replied, "I don't know, boss, but they sure got a lot of balls."

Tony tucked the envelope he was given into his jacket and instructed his emissary to leave. He sat down bewildered by what he was told and wondered what his next move should be.

TWELVE

Enzo quite often took time to visit his *paesans*. All of them were immigrant men, just like him, who had come to America in search of a better life. While none of them had become quite as successful as Enzo, they all had made a better life for themselves and their families in America. A few of them worked for Enzo from time to time.

Enzo particularly liked visiting his *paesan* Dominick, who had chosen to settle in Canada instead of the United States. Dominick and his family lived just across the border in Fort Erie, Ontario. During the early spring, Enzo would go fishing with Dominick in the Niagara River, dipping for smelts during the annual spring smelt runs in the river. The men would net bushel upon bushels of smelts in one night of fishing. Enzo would bring two to three bushels back across the border with him. Whenever the customs inspectors at the border would ask to check his trunk, they would immediately tell him to close it after getting a view and a whiff of the smelly cargo.

Dominick was an experienced burglar and had recently hit a jewelry store in a nearby city. His loot was more than he could dump off in his area and so he asked Enzo for some help in selling it off. The loot contained precious stones, as well as some expensive timepieces.

After their next fishing outing, Enzo wrapped several of the items in plastic and placed them in the bottom of a bushel. He then dumped a bushel full of smelts into the same bushel covering the precious stones and timepieces. He headed back across the border to the States, smelly and precious cargo in his trunk. This time he was a bit nervous as he approached the customs inspector.

The inspector keyed his plate number into his computer to check for any outstanding warrants. He then questioned Enzo. "Where were you born?" he asked?

"Sicily," replied Enzo.

"Citizen of what country?" he then asked.

"U.S.," Enzo replied.

"Bringing anything back?" the inspector asked.

"I got some fish, some smelts," responded Enzo.

"Let's have a look," said the inspector.

Enzo popped open the trunk.

"Whoa! You gonna eat all those?" asked the inspector.

"I give lots to my friends," Enzo said to him.

"Okay, close the trunk, it stinks," the inspector said, waving his hand in front of his nose. He waived Enzo on through the checkpoint and Enzo was on his way home.

Enzo turned the stolen goods over to Nunzio to see if he could sell them. Within a day, all the loot had been sold. Nunzio called Enzo to give him the news.

"Hey, Pops, I sold it all. I got the asking price, too," he told Enzo over the phone.

"Good, Dominick is going to be very happy," Enzo, replied.

"Got any more?" Nunzio asked.

"I check next time I go there, I let you know," said Enzo.

The following week Enzo returned to once again visit his *paesan,* Dominick. He brought Alex along in hopes they could spend some time fishing together. As they sat out on the front porch with Dominick, Enzo handed him an envelope containing seven thousand dollars.

"Open it," he said to Dominick.

Dominick looked inside and counted the money.

"*Minghia*," Dominick said with a smile on his face. "That's better than we can get here." He then took one thousand dollars and gave it back to Enzo.

"Thank you very much," Enzo said. "Do you have anymore to sell?" he asked.

"I can get more," replied Dominick. "You know who is in Toronto?"

"Who?" asked Enzo.

"Rocco San Marco and his son, Nino," said Dominick.

"My good friend, Nino?" asked Enzo.

"Yes, your friend, Nino," said Dominick.

As Dominick and Enzo continued their discussion, Enzo learned that Nino was involved in some of the burglaries, as well as hijackings north of the border. Enzo realized there was a bounty of merchandise to be sold not readily available to him in the U.S. The question remained, how could they get it out of Canada and into the states? Alex sat quietly listening.

On the way home Alex said to his father, "They have a lot of merchandise you can't seem to get over here. Maybe too much, it won't fit in the bottom of a bushel."

"How did you know about that?" asked Enzo.

Alex laughed. "Nunzio told me. I've got an idea I think might help."

"Okay, what is it?" asked Enzo.

"My friend, Mel, his uncle has a house right on Millers Creek. The house has a boat dock," said Alex.

"Where is this Millers Creek?" asked Enzo.

"On the Canadian side, it flows into the Niagara River," said Alex.

"So what, he's got a house that goes into the river," Enzo said.

"Well, you could use the dock to load the merchandise in a boat. Then at night, when it's dark, you have a boat from this side meet their boat in the middle of the river. You transfer the goods from one boat to another and voila. All done under the cover of darkness," Alex said to his father. "Maybe you have some stuff they could sell for you. Oh, and one more thing, you should get at least forty percent."

"What didn't your brother tell you?" Enzo asked. "I'll check out this idea of yours. Let's see if it makes sense, first. We should know who patrols the river and things like that."

"I'll introduce you to Mel's uncle," Alex said. "I know he will go for it. He is having trouble making payments on the house in Canada."

"He is?" asked Enzo.

"Yeah," said Alex. "You could offer to make the payments for him. I'll set it up for Friday at six o'clock. That will give you time to check things out.

Enzo drove Alex home and pulled into the driveway. He stuffed five hundred dollars into his shirt pocket before Alex got out of the car.

"What's that for?" asked Alex.

"Payment for advice," replied Enzo.

"Like a *consiglieri*?" asked Alex.

"Don't get carried away," said Enzo.

After meeting with Mel's uncle, Enzo drove over to Dominick's across the border. He informed him that he had established a way for them to smuggle stolen goods between the two countries. Dominick was very receptive to the idea and both men agreed on their new business venture. It was also agreed that the seller would receive forty percent and the supplier sixty percent. This would keep things even on both sides.

Before long, the CAN-AM pipeline, as it came to be called, was bringing in thousands of dollars a week. Enzo had established himself in a new business, one with international reach. As was the case with his other dealings, he was very generous to all those involved in the operation.

Enzo went to Toronto to visit his friend, Nino, whom he had not seen since he left Belgium. Until the time Dominick had told him that Nino was in Canada, Enzo had no idea what his old friend had been doing or even where he was. In his pursuit of building his empire, Enzo had lost touch with many of the important things in his past.

During his visit, Enzo learned that Nino also had a source for counterfeit and bootleg merchandise. Most of the counterfeit and bootleg merchandise was coming from Asia. It was much easier for the smugglers to bring the loot in through Canadian ports than through US ports. Enzo secured a steady stream of goods for himself by agreeing to pay for merchandise up front, before delivery was made. By doing so, he avoided having to give the smugglers any type of percentage after the sale. He was now free to set his own prices to his buyers. He agreed to pay Nino ten percent of the initial buy price as a fee for hooking him up with the smugglers. Nino was agreeable.

Enzo also learned that Nino had sources for other contraband, such as illegal drugs. The fact that Nino was even involved with drug dealers angered Enzo. For this reason Enzo preferred to pay the counterfeit smugglers up front and not through Nino.

Enzo did not allow any of his own people to be involved in drugs. He believed that the drug business was too risky a business venture and ultimately ended up hurting innocent people.

By not forwarding large sums of money through Nino, he avoided ever having a significant money trail that could be tied to drugs. He even sent Nino's commission through Dominick, to minimize the risk of being tied to drug dealers.

Enzo knew that this business that he was now in posed some risks. Any time there were large amounts of money exchanging hands in a covert fashion, there was the risk for someone in the pipeline to become greedy and attempt to cheat the others. When it was discovered, it usually meant a severe beating for the perpetrator and, in some instances, even death.

A year had now passed since Enzo established the CAN-AM. pipeline. Dominick had suspected that one of his sources for stolen gems, named Frank Rickman, had been substituting inferior quality stones for the high valued stones he had been paying for. Dominick had the stones checked out by a gemologist and confirmed his suspicion. After further investigation, he learned that Frank was also trying to sell the high valued stones himself and pocket the monies. This angered Dominick.

Dominick had invited Enzo to come over to Canada to do some dipping for smelts. Enzo invited Alex and Nunzio to join him so they could make it a father and son outing. Both of his sons agreed to join him, but Nunzio had to cancel at the last minute because of a problem at a job site. Alex drove across the Peace Bridge with Enzo to Dominick's house. When they arrived they found Dominick had been drinking quite heavily. He was joined by his brother-in law, Vito, who, while he had consumed a fair amount himself, was still coherent. The four men drove to a spot on the river near the International Railroad Bridge.

On the way to the river Dominick had filled Enzo in on the stone-swapping situation. He told him that the person involved was coming to the river to deliver some gems that very night.

It was a cold March night and the ice was flowing out of the lake and down the river at a rapid pace. Dominick had hopped onto some big boulders and made his way to a large boulder in the river about thirty yards away from the rest of the men who had remained on the shore. Dominick was so drunk he had a difficult time dipping his long net into the river and avoiding the chunks of ice that were flowing down the river.

"*Soonamabitch*," he would yell when he got ice tangled in his net.

"Dominick, *you gonna* drown, you crazy bastard," Enzo yelled out to him. "Come on back here with us. I *no gonna* come and *geta you* ass if you fall in"

About thirty minutes after they had arrived, the headlights from a car coming down the hill towards the river appeared. Dominick looked up and said to the others, "It's him. Send him out here when he comes down."

When Frank arrived Enzo told him to go and get Dominick off the rocks.

Dominick yelled out, "Hey, Frankie, you got my stones? Come over here and help me get back." Frank hopped across the boulders and made his way over to Dominick. The two men sat on the boulder for a few moments, talking. They both stood up to make their way back to the shore. Frankie led the way. As he jumped back to the next boulder he turned to wait for Dominick. Dominick now followed.

Dominick said to Frank, "I think I dropped my keys."

"Where?" asked Frank.

"Over there," said Dominick as he pointed down to the edge of the boulder.

Frank bent over to look for the keys. Just then Dominick pulled a revolver from his jacket and shot Frank twice in the back of the head. The others on shore were astonished.

Alex, who was sitting on a rock, stood up immediately and yelled out, "What the hell!"

As Frank's body tumbled into the river Dominick said, " I kill the *soonamabitch*."

Alex began to shout to the others, "Are you fucking guys crazy? Holy shits, look what he did." He turned to Enzo, "Dad, what the hell is this bullshit?" he asked.

Dominick slowly made his way back to shore.

Enzo walked over to him, grabbed him and threw him down to the ground. "You didn't have to kill him, you stupid bastard," he said. "What the hell is the matter with you? And you do this mess in front of my son. Goddamn you."

Alex began walking back towards the car. He said to Enzo, "Let's get out of here."

In the course of all the commotion, Dominick in his polluted state refused to get up and insisted on lying down and sleeping. Vito asked for Enzo's help to get Dominick to the car.

Enzo steadfastly refused. "Fuck him! I don't care if he drowns. Let him stay there," he said to Vito.

Vito once again pleaded with Enzo. Enzo eventually gave in and helped load Dominick into the car. Alex, who was by now sitting in the car, refused to get out of the car and assist the others.

After dropping Dominick and Vito off at their homes, Enzo and Alex drove back to Buffalo.

"I can't believe he did that," Enzo said to Alex. "It was not necessary, just not necessary." "I can't believe he just shot the guy like that," Alex said. "They're going to find this guy's body at the bottom of the falls in about a week."

Enzo looked at his son and said, "This is not how I want to do my business." He shrugged his shoulders. "It's unfortunate, but sometimes this shit happens."

As they pulled into the driveway, Enzo hugged his son and said to him, "I'm sorry you had to see that."

"Yeah, me too," Alex replied. "I'm tired. I'm going to bed," he said to his father as he walked into the house.

THIRTEEN

Alex awoke early the next day and drove over to Nunzio's house for breakfast. Stefano had decided that morning to come over, as well. It seemed Stefano was more like a brother to Nunzio and Alex than he was an uncle. The three had been very close since Stefano had arrived in America as a fourteen-year-old boy along with Raimondo. Even though he was only five years older than Nunzio, Stefano always looked after his nephews to make certain nothing bad ever happened to them.

As the three men were sitting down at the kitchen table drinking coffee, Nunzio's wife, Rosie, came down the stairs and entered the kitchen.

"Good morning, fellas, what are we having this morning?" asked Rosie.

"Ah no, don't bother, Rosie, we're okay," Alex replied.

"Yeah, we're good, Rosie, don't bother," said Stefano.

Rosie took a frying pan out of the cupboard and twirling it in her hands asked the threesome, "You want bacon or sausage with your eggs, fellas?"

Alex replied, "Sausage."

Stefano replied, "Bacon."

Nunzio laughed, looked at Rosie, and said, "Better make them both."

Nunzio had met Rosie while in college and they married shortly after graduation. Rosie loved cooking for the guys and they loved hanging out at Nunzio's so they could get some of her good cooking.

Stefano had no intention of settling down with any woman. He still lived at home with his parents and enjoyed the freedom his single lifestyle afforded him. When asked when are you going to settle down he would reply, "When I've had all the pussy in Buffalo, then I'll know which is the best."

Stefano had a very short fuse and had little fear of anyone or anything. He always seemed to be searching for his way in life, but could never really find it. He was happy working for Enzo's development company but even happier that Enzo had included him in his new business ventures. His personality and boldness made him a perfect fit in the business. If he had one downfall it was that he would rather settle a disagreement by busting up someone's face than discussing the matter. He had little patience for negotiating or words. He was a man of action, usually violent.

On one occasion, Stefano, Alex and Nunzio were having lunch at their local hangout the Your Host Restaurant. Stefano had made a flirtatious comment to a beautiful girl that was sitting at the counter. He did not realize that she was with another man who had left the table to use the restroom. When he returned the woman told him about Stefano's comments. Her partner turned to Stefano and made some disparaging comments to him. Before long, they were outside quarreling when the man suddenly pulled a small caliber handgun on Stefano. As Alex ducked for cover Stefano stood perfectly still and said to the handgun-toting man, "If you don't pull the trigger I'm going to make you eat that fuckin' thing." The man thought better of it and attempted to put the gun back in his pocket and walk away. Before he could get the gun put away, Stefano had disarmed him and struck him in the mouth with the handgun repeatedly. After knocking out several of his front teeth, he then proceeded to bite off his ear lobe. Nunzio jumped in to pull Stefano away. Alex stood horrified. If Stefano did have one redeeming quality it was that he was a very generous person and he was very loyal to his family.

Alex was somewhat undecided about his future career goals after high school and decided to attend a community college. Enzo was pushing hard for him to consider medicine as a field of study. He was still living at home with Enzo, Louise and Catalina while attending college. Enzo tried his hardest to keep Alex away from the family business in an attempt to keep him focused on his studies.

Alex spent a lot of time with his brother, Nunzio, and Uncle Stefano. Being a close-knit family there were not many things that were not openly discussed, so that being the case, Alex was always very well-informed of all the family business matters, both legal and illegal. He was also never reserved in his opinions or suggestions that he would offer. Nunzio and Stefano would always listen closely to what Alex had to say and welcomed his suggestions. That was not the case with Enzo. He often chided Nunzio and Stefano for being too open with Alex on matters concerning the family business. "Why do you have to tell him everything?" he would often ask Nunzio and Stefano. "If you pull him away from his studies, you gonn*a pissa* me off! Let him finish school."

Alex and Nunzio were no strangers to hard work. Both worked odd jobs from the sixth grade through their high school years cutting grass, painting and tilling gardens in the neighborhood for spending money. Having acquired forged documents with Enzo's help both had landed well-paying part-time jobs at the Statler Hotel. Neither had reached the required age of eighteen when they were employed. The hours were long and the work was difficult, but it prepared them both for what would lie ahead in their lives.

While Enzo did pay college tuition for his children, there were not many other luxuries provided to them when they reached a working age. He did make an automobile available to them for transportation to school, which the boys had to share. With both of them in college at the same time this was sometimes tricky, especially when schedules did not correspond. At times, one of them would have to carpool with friends in order to get to school. Alex and Nunzio always seemed to be able to work it out and it seldom became a source of contention. Gas was their responsibility, as well, and so was keeping up the routine maintenance of the vehicles, such as oil changes and car washes. All the family vehicles were washed routinely on Saturday mornings. It was almost a ritual to Enzo and he very much enjoyed his sons participating in it.

Enzo was so proud of one car in particular, an Oldsmobile Ninety-Eight that he had purchased brand-new. He had wanted a Cadillac, but Louise was opposed to having a Caddy in the driveway. It was a *tizzun* car she would say. He kept this car immaculately clean, inside and out. The car had a black leather interior and the slightest spec of dust was easily noticeable on the seats.

On one particular Friday evening while Alex was in college, he had asked if he could borrow the car to go out with some friends. Since Nunzio had taken the other vehicle earlier, that left only the Olds for Alex. Since he had no plans for the evening, Enzo agreed to let Alex borrow his pride and joy. "Don't get it dirty," he said to Alex as he headed out the door.

Alex left his house and headed to the south side of town to meet up with Nancy, a girl he had met in his anatomy class at the community college. She worked as a cashier at a local supermarket and was getting off work at 7 p.m. Alex met her at the supermarket at the end of her shift. They decided to go and have a beer together at The Jolly Roger, a local neighborhood tavern. After drinking their beer it was off to Seneca Town Park for some extracurricular activities. They parked in a dark, secluded area of the park, near a baseball diamond. After about thirty minutes of necking and petting inside the car, Alex not wanting to dirty his father's car asked Nancy to go outside with him to continue their playful encounter. It was a bit chilly outside and Nancy was unwilling to undress in the cold of the night. She told Alex that if he wanted to "stick it in her" it would have to be inside the car on the back seat. Alex agreed and they headed back to the car and climbed into the back seat. Within minutes Nancy had taken off her pants and the two were fucking like two wild dogs in heat. The car windows had become so fogged up that Alex used his tee shirt to wipe them down so they could drive out of the park.

Alex took Nancy home and returned to his home. He parked the car in the usual spot in the driveway, went inside and slipped off to bed. What he had not realized was that while rolling around in the grass in the park he and Nancy had rolled onto some areas that had been freshly topsoiled and seeded. The dirt from the park was all over their clothing and now also all over the inside of Enzo's car.

The next morning Enzo was up early, as was his routine on Saturday mornings. He decided to wait a while to wash the cars, as that morning was a bit chilly. He wandered outside with his cup of coffee and walked down the steps to the driveway. He noticed some mud on the tires of the Olds and decided to investigate further. He opened the door looked inside and exclaimed, "holy *fuckina chit.*" He quickly headed back to the house, yelling for Alex, who was still in bed sleeping. He reached Alex's room and tore the covers off of Alex while he was still in bed.

"Where *da fucka you* go *lasta* night?" he asked in his Italian accent.

"I went out with my friends," Alex replied.

"*Bulla* shit, you *friendsa,* my ass," Enzo said. "There's footprints on the roof inside the car, and the windows look like somebody *wipa da* mud on them." He continued his tirade. "You *gonna geta* up *anda* clean. I *no gonna* clean," Alex quickly arose and headed outside to clean up his mess.

Nunzio climbed out of bed to see what the commotion was all about. "What's going on?" he asked.

"You brother screw some *putana* in my car *lasta* night and *maka da* mess," Enzo replied.

"What, he left his mess on the seats?" Nunzio asked.

"No, its full of dust and dirt, filthy," said Enzo. Nunzio went outside to see for himself. Alex was filling a pail with soap and water as Nunzio looked inside the car.

"*Whoa bro*, who did you fuck last night, a farmers daughter?" Nunzio asked. "Holy shit, look at this, footprints on the ceiling, a long legged fuckin' farmer she was, too," Nunzio said as he noticed the footprints on the roof of the interior. Nunzio laughed as he gave his little brother more grief about last night's encounter. He began to walk away and came back to the car as Alex had hosed down the exterior.

"Know who I nailed last night?" he asked Alex.

"Who?" Alex asked.

"Diane, the whale," said Nunzio.

"No shit. Finally, huh?" said Alex.

"Yup. The shrimp got to swim inside the whale," said Nunzio.

Alex finished washing the car and went back inside the house. Louise had breakfast waiting on the table. Enzo, Louise, Alex and Nunzio sat down at the table to eat the breakfast Louise had prepared.

As they were finishing, Louise looked at Alex and said, "I heard your father say you had sex in his car last night. You are a pig! If you make somebody pregnant you are not going to be able to study no more." Alex laughed. "It's not funny," she said to him.

"Listen to your mama," Nunzio said to Alex laughingly.

Alex arose from the table and placed his dish in the sink. He turned to Louise who was still seated at the table with Nunzio and asked, "Did Nunz tell you he screwed the whale last night?" Nunzio sat in silence.

Louise turned to Nunzio and said, "You two, you are both pigs. Both my sons are pigs!" Louise stood up and left the room shaking her head.

Catalina was very close to her brothers, Alex and Nunzio. Although younger than her brothers, she spent a considerable amount of time with them while she was growing up. While she did not actually dislike her Uncle Stefano, she kept her distance from him. She believed he, as she would put it, "has a screw loose upstairs." His behavior was too unpredictable for her.

Catalina was much more reserved, much quieter than the rest of her family. She was very religious and practiced her catholic faith regularly. She attended a small Catholic college, graduating with a degree in criminal justice. After college she went to work for the county court system as a legal aide. While she had dated several different men, she remained single, waiting for the perfect man to walk into her life. About the most trouble she ever gave her parents was getting drunk at her sixteenth birthday party and throwing up in her bedroom in the middle of the night.

She stayed very close with her mother even through her college years. This, at a time when most of her peers were distancing themselves from their parents. They were not only mother and daughter; they were also very good friends. They spent time shopping together and even went to movies together. Catalina filled a need in Louise's life that Enzo seemingly had no time for. She was well aware of the problems between Louise and Enzo, and while it tore her up inside, she never discussed the situation with either of them.

While she did not fully comprehend what it was that Enzo actually did for a living, she did understand he was involved in illegal activities. She refused to believe he would ever physically harm anyone. She regarded what she did know of his illegal activities as harmless. She adored her father for what he had accomplished, despite being a poorly educated immigrant. She would often comment that people with MBA's were not as accomplished as her father. She remained well-sheltered from any details of the family business and chose to ignore many of the things she did find out.

Catalina trusted her brothers to look after her. If there was any indication that anyone would even come close to offending or harming her, her brothers were always there to send a warning to the offending party. On one occasion while Catalina was still in college, she had attended a football game at the university with some of her classmates. As is the case at most college football games, many of the fans were a bit drunk at the game. One in particular was a young man in her philosophy class named Albert, who had attended the game with Catalina and her friends. While in his state of intoxication he decided to put his hands up Catalina's shirt, an action she very much objected to. When she screamed at him and asked what the hell he was doing, he replied, "keeping my hands warm."

It wasn't long before word got back to Alex and Nunzio about what had happened at the football game. Despite the fact that Catalina said she had taken care of the situation, Nunzio decided to take action to preserve his sister's honor.

Albert worked part-time at a local pizzeria, making pizzas and subs. At the end of every shift he was required to clean the food prep area to prepare for the next day. After cleaning the kitchen area he would take the trash to the dumpster behind the building. Five days after the incident at the football game, Nunzio was waiting for Albert behind the building. As Albert carried the trash to the dumpster, he was greeted by Nunzio and Raul.

"Hello, hot hands," Nunzio said to Albert as the two men approached him.

"Excuse me," replied Albert.

Just then Raul grabbed him around the neck and wrestled him to the ground. Nunzio now placed his foot on Albert's head, pushing it to the pavement.

"Did you have fun grabbing my sister's knockers at the game?" he asked.

Albert screamed out in pain. "I'm sorry, I'm sorry, I was drunk, it won't happen again, I promise!" He began to cry. "Please don't kill me, please." Nunzio stomped down on his head repeatedly causing him to lose consciousness.

"Let's put him in the garbage," Raul said.

"Help me lift him up," Nunzio said. The two men lifted the unconscious Albert and threw him into the dumpster.

"You piece of garbage, that's where you belong," Nunzio said to him as his body hit the slimy, smelly trash in the dumpster.

Enzo and Louise admired their children for being so close to each other. Despite the fact that their own relationship had long been in trouble, they always encouraged their children to love and respect each other. They had done an exceptional job in keeping them close. Not a day went by that they were not in contact with each other.

FOURTEEN

Enzo wanted only the best for his children and the best meant studying hard and getting a good education. He had done so much to make his children's lives so much more comfortable than what he had experienced, himself, as a child. Here in America, there was no threat of war as he had experienced in his childhood, and the opportunities that came with a good education would provide a comfortable living for a lifetime. This was his dream. Perhaps one of his children would become a doctor, perhaps another a lawyer, maybe even a senator. Here they would escape the poverty and the ravishes of war that he had experienced as a child. He was so proud to tell his *peasans* that one of his children would one day be a doctor or a lawyer. There was also the hope that none of them would have to become a part of this 'thing', that he was now a part of with little hope for escape. He wanted for them to have a nobler calling. It was not a pleasant feeling to always have to look over your shoulder and never know who you could trust.

After two years at a community college, Alex applied to a local university and was accepted into the pre-med program. Nothing could have made Enzo happier.

"When you become a doctor you won't have to dig ditches for a living like I did," Enzo would tell Alex. "People will respect you and besides, I will get medical care for free," he would tell his son.

As Alex left for his first day at the university, his mother embraced him with tears in her eyes. "My son, the future doctor," she whispered in his ear. "Good luck, son," she shouted as he drove away. As Alex drove towards the campus he thought to himself how studying to become a doctor was really not in his heart. He had wanted so desperately to be a business major. He did not have the heart to disappoint his father, so he went about his business and followed the course that his father had set for him.

Alex entered his first classroom at the university. Across the board was written:

"WELCOME… THIS IS MICROBIOLOGY… MR. RITTER." He found a seat next to a window and sat down. He pulled a notebook from his book bag and titled the first page "Micro 101/Ritter. He briefly glanced at the girl sitting next to him and very courteously smiled and said hello. He turned to look back to the front of the class and saw a tall bald man in a sport coat and tie enter the room.

"Good morning," the tall, imposing figure greeted his students.

"Good morning," several of them replied.

"Welcome to Microbiology and good luck," he responded. Many of the students giggled.

"There are three rules to success in this class," he said. "Come to class, complete the assignments and never, but never get behind in your memorization."

Alex copiously wrote down the professor's instructions.

"Do you always take such detailed notes?" whispered the young girl sitting next to Alex.

" I have to, it is how I learn," responded Alex.

"Umm-umm," Mr. Ritter looking at Alex said, "you have a better chance at learning if you listen and don't talk in my class. Stay focused up here."

"Sorry, sir," replied Alex.

The professor continued with his first day's speech on expectations and a brief outline of the course. After assigning the first three chapters of the book as a reading assignment before the next class, he dismissed the class.

Alex placed his textbook and notebook into his book bag and got up out of his seat. As he started his walk to the door he heard a voice say,

"Sorry about that earlier, I didn't mean to get us in trouble on the first day." It was the girl who had questioned his note taking.

"Oh, don't worry about it. It's really not a problem," replied Alex.

"I'm Gabriella," she said to Alex.

"I'm Alex," he replied.

"What's your next class?" she asked.

"Anatomy," he replied.

"Me, too," she said. "Want to walk together?" Gabriella asked.

"Sure," replied Alex. They headed to their next class together.

They both soon discovered that they both not only shared the same major, but also were in all the same classes. They agreed to be study partners, helping each other prepare for term papers and study for exams, as well.

Gabriella had always struggled as a student and having someone like Alex as a study partner would make things much easier for her. Her father would be very pleased, as well. She could not wait to go home and tell her father about her first day and about having met Alex. Because she was somewhat shy, she had always had a problem in making friends and keeping them. She was determined to not let this happen to her in college. She felt she had hit a home run with Alex. She was confident her father would approve.

After a few days of studying together after school, Gabriella invited Alex to come to her home on Sunday evening to prepare for an exam. Alex accepted and told her he would be there at approximately 6 p.m. It was agreed they would order pizza to munch on while studying. After giving Alex directions to her house, they parted company.

Alex arrived a few minutes early on Sunday evening. He rang the doorbell and was greeted by a man. It was Gabriella's father.

"How are you doing? I'm Tony, Tony Riccio, Gabriella's father," he said to Alex.

Alex smiled and replied as he shook his hand. "I'm Alex, Alex Melina, nice to meet you, sir." "Come in, Gabriella is in the library. Go straight and turn right at the second door," her father said.

"Thank you," replied Alex.

Gabriella and Alex studied together for about two hours when Alex decided it was time to go. Gabriella walked him to the door. As they stood in the doorway chatting, her father came over to Alex and asked, "Alex, are you related to the Melinas on Hope Street?"

"I sure am, sir. I live there," replied Alex.

"Is your father Enzo?" asked her father.

"That's him," said Alex.

"I know your father very well. We are somewhat business associates from the union," her father said.

"Oh, Daddy, you and the union," murmured Gabriella.

Alex now spoke, "You know, I knew your family name sounded familiar, but I never gave it a second thought." He giggled. "My dad mentions you all the time. Wait 'til I tell him. Cool." "Tell your father next time you come, for him to come, too. We can talk some business," Gabriella's father said to Alex.

"Business and the union, that's all my father knows," Gabriella said to Alex.

"Hey little girl, it's going to pay your way through med school, no complaining," her father shouted to her.

"I'm no little girl," replied Gabriella.

"You're my little girl," her father said to her as he turned towards her, lifted her and gave her a hug.

"Daddy stop, you're embarrassing me," Gabriella said as she darted out of his reach.

Alex stood there watching and smiling. "Got to go," he said as he walked to his car and drove away.

Alex went home, but never mentioned to his family that he had been studying with Tony Riccio's daughter. He sensed from Tony's reaction to his daughter that he was somewhat protective, but also very compromising with her. He thought to himself, *Maybe I could get close enough to make this thing between my father and Tony work.* What he knew he could not afford to do was put himself in a risky position with Tony. He decided he would continue studying with Gabriella and get closer to Tony. If he could get Tony to really like him, that could make things easier after a while between Tony and his father. For now he would not mention it to his family; he would wait until he could deliver the big fish and then tell his father.

Alex enjoyed studying with Gabriella and they became close friends, sharing intimate details of their lives. Alex not really sure how much Gabriella knew about her father's business, was very careful never to mention the union or family business dealings with Gabriella. She seemed after all, not very interested in it anyway.

Gabriella always dressed rather conservatively and wore wire-rimmed glasses, which did nothing to accentuate her beautiful hazel eyes. She had very full lips, high cheekbones and after having her braces removed she bore a million dollar smile. Alex realized that underneath those baggy, frumpy clothes was a beautiful voluptuous body. He had often times fantasized about being with her but was afraid that a wrong move could mean jeopardizing the relationship he had begun to build with her father. He realized that he had begun to have feelings for her. He was determined to be the one who brokered the agreement between Tony and his own father and had to keep his raging hormones under control for the good of the family.

Gabriella had begun to notice Alex, as well. His wit made her feel so much at ease and she was awed by his intelligence. He was charming and courteous and always made her laugh. For the first time in her life she felt attracted sexually to a man. She knew deep down inside she desired him, but couldn't break through her shyness to tell him. She felt comfortable discussing other aspects of her life with him, but not her feelings of desire. She felt a sense of confusion with the new feelings and emotions she had acquired. She was dealing with a potpourri of questions in her mind. Would Alex reject her, and if they did become intimate would Alex then lose interest? There was also the question of her father and his feelings. She loved Tony so much and while she felt so safe with him, she at times felt smothered by him. It seemed at times that Tony would not allow her to grow up. Her mother had died of cancer two years earlier and she was all Tony had left. She was afraid of not meeting the expectations he had laid out for her and did not want to disappoint him. Until now Tony had received all of her attention. Tony and Gabriella seemed inseparable at times, but that was all about to change. Gabriella had become a woman with womanly desires.

Her desire for Alex grew stronger as the semester wore on and she decided she would take precautions in case her and Alex did become intimate. Knowing that she could not visit any of the local OB/GYN physicians for fear her father would find out, she visited a physician out of town and obtained a prescription for birth control.

The following month Tony was away for a weekend business trip to the Bahamas and she invited Alex over for pizza. That morning she had put new sheets on her bed in anticipation of what would be her first event. She had thought it through and she was ready. This would be the night.

On the way over to Gabriella's, Alex had decided to reveal his feelings to Gabriella. He could not be near her any longer without her knowing how he felt. He would make his statement and be done with it. As he drove along he noticed a street vendor selling bouquets of flowers. He stopped and bought the brightest bouquet he saw on the cart. He was now headed directly to Gabriella's. Just as he pulled into the driveway the pizza delivery arrived, as well. He paid the deliveryman for the pizza and rang the doorbell.

"Pizza, pizza," he shouted as Gabriella came to the door. "*You lika pepperoni ana da cheez?*" he asked jokingly.

She smiled at him and said, "Come on in, silly."

He followed her into the kitchen. She never noticed the flower bouquet he was holding behind his back. "These are for you," he said.

Surprised, she now wore a smile, which beamed from ear to ear. She turned to him and kissed him on the cheek. She turned away for a moment to find a vase in the cabinet behind her and put some water from the sink in the vase. Alex tore off the wrapping on the bouquet and pulled out a beautiful partially opened red rose from the bouquet. He handed her the bouquet and she placed the flowers in the vase. Alex grabbed her right hand and pulled her close to him. His heart was racing as he was searching for the words to say. Gabriella felt weakness in her legs as she drew closer to him.

As he handed her the rose, he said to her, "This flower, my dear, is for the prettiest pre-med student at the university. Do you see how close and tight the petals in this rose are?"

"*Yeeess*," Gabriella replied.

"That's like me and you, real close." He now pulled her tightly against him. "And real tight," he whispered in her ear.

His heart raced even faster as he was drawn to her now glossy eyes. It seemed as though some magnetic force was drawing them even tighter together. Gabriella could barely stand on her legs as they began to quiver. Her heart began to race and it almost seemed as if she would soon be gasping for air. Just as she opened her lips to catch a deep breath, Alex pressed his lips against hers. She exhaled through her nose as she now pressed her lips even tighter against Alex's. Alex could feel his penis begin to swell as he placed his hands on her buttocks and drew her pelvis against his body. She felt a warm, wet sensation in her vagina and was turned on by feeling his hardness against her. Alex separated her lips with his tongue and put his tongue in her mouth. She felt his tongue on hers and began to swirl her tongue around his. Alex rubbed his hardness against her. Gabriella moaned quietly. She could feel the sweat rolling down the small of her back and his hand now traveling through the inside of the back of her blouse.

With both of his hands now inside the back of her blouse, Alex gently caressed her back with his fingertips bringing up the sweat from the small of her back with his fingertips to between her shoulder blades. His hand traveled up to her breasts and as he caressed them gently her nipples began to harden. Alex then slipped her blouse over her head and began to kiss her nipples. Gabriella began to melt with passion.

With his mouth still on her breasts, she began to backpedal towards the library. Alex shuffled his feet and followed, never separating himself from her breasts. Once in the library Gabriella pushed the ottoman against the oversize lounger in the corner of the room. She fell backwards into the chair with Alex seemingly on top of her. Alex now reached down and shoved his hand into her panties as they positioned themselves in the center of the chair. He rubbed his fingers against her clitoris as Gabriella began to breathe faster and moan even louder. She slipped his shirt over his head and kissed him on the chest. Alex now took her hand and rubbed it against his penis on the outside of his pants.

"I'm dying to slip this inside you," Alex whispered to her.

"I'm dying to have it inside me," she whispered back as she unbuckled his trousers and slipped them off his body. She could now see his hard, bulging penis through his underwear as he put his hands under her and slipped off her pants and underwear.

Alex was now looking down at her unbelievably beautiful body which was now completely uncovered beneath him. Still wearing his underwear, he laid directly on top of her. He rubbed his bulging penis against her vagina as she closed her eyes and let her head slip back into the cushion. Her moans grew louder and closer together. He inserted the fingers of his right hand into her vagina and used his left hand to pull off his underwear. He separated her thighs with his knees and drew himself close to her. Gabriella had tilted her head back and was biting her lower lip. Alex could see the droplets of sweat on her forehead and under her chin. He slowly and gently slipped his penis inside her and swayed gently back and forth several times. He then thrust deeply inside her. A virgin until now, she grimaced slightly in pain as his penis slid further inside her. As Alex thrust back and forth, she felt a sudden tingle in her spine. Her toes began to tingle as well until she felt this tremendous tingling throughout her entire body.

"OH GOD, UMMMM, OH GOD," she screamed as she felt all of her muscles begin to tighten. Her head tilted back even further as she felt this tremendous burst of ecstasy envelope her entire body. "AHHHHHHH," she screamed in ecstasy, biting on her lower lip as she reached the peak of her orgasm. She could hear Alex breathing harder with every thrust, as well, until he, too, let out a moan as he seemingly exploded inside her. She felt the warm sensation of his cum as he ejaculated deep inside her. As they both fell back to a resting position, with Alex still on top, she could feel warmth and moistness as his penis exited her body.

Their bodies were seemingly stuck together from sweat as their breathing began to slow down. Alex caressed her face and kissed her cheeks. Gabriella was now gazing at the ceiling as she began to feel her muscles relax. She could still feel the tingling in her spine and toes as Alex rolled off her and lay to her side.

He put his arm around her kissed her forehead and gazed into her eyes. She snuggled close to him as they both closed their eyes and fell asleep. Not a single word was spoken. Alex awoke about an hour later covered by a small blanket. Gabriella was now fully dressed and standing over him.

"We never did get to the pizza," she said to him. "I'll heat it in the oven," she said as she exited the room.

Alex slipped on his clothes and proceeded to the kitchen. " Don't get it too hot," he said to her, as he entered the kitchen. He went directly to her and put his arms around her. "Are you okay with this?" he asked her.

"What, the pizza?" she asked.

"Not the pizza. You know… what just happened in there," Alex replied.

"Alex, this was my first time ever. Until then I was a virgin. It was everything I had hoped it would be. And you know something else?" she asked.

"No, what?" Alex replied.

"It was special because it was with someone I trust and care for very much. Someone I think I am falling in love with," she whispered to Alex.

Alex held her tighter as he searched for the right words to say. He had not planned on falling in love, but he could not deny his feelings any longer. "I feel the same way," he told her.

She grabbed him by the hand, led him to the table and they enjoyed their pizza together.

In the months that followed Alex and Gabriella spent more and more time together. On campus, they were almost inseparable. Between school, a part-time job and seeing Gabriella, Alex spent little time at home. Louise had even remarked to Alex that the only time he came home was to shower and sleep. Alex had told Enzo and Louise about his friendship with Gabriella in early October. It was now only a few weeks from Christmas and Alex had gone to the mall with Louise to help pick out a Christmas gift for Enzo. While there, Alex had asked Louise for help in picking out a ruby pendant for Gabriella. Louise waited until they had gone out to the car to initiate a conversation concerning Gabriella.

"I guess this means you are pretty serious about this girl," she said to Alex. "But why do you not speak to me about it? You always talk with me about things, but not this time, why?"

Alex replied. "Mom, I did not plan to get serious with this one, it just happened. I think I love her. Besides, she is Tony Riccio's daughter, I don't know how to tell Dad or if he would approve."

Louise stroked her son's cheek and said to him, "You *no worry about you* father, I talk to him, but Friday you bring her to dinner at the house."

That Friday Gabriella came to the Melina house for dinner. Enzo was courteous, although somewhat uneasy. Louise immediately bonded with Gabriella and they spent several hours in the sunroom talking mostly about Gabriella and her mother.

Alex and Enzo had gone into the basement to the workshop where Alex approached Enzo with a proposition. "Dad, I think I have a solution to the problem you and Tony have," Alex said nervously to Enzo.

"What do you know about my problem?" Enzo asked. "You should worry about your school work and not my business," he said angrily.

Waving his hands Alex responded. "Hear me out on this, just listen for a minute! If you don't clarify with Tony what action you get and what action the other guys get, you're going to cross over with these guys again and people are going to start shooting at each other and all kinds of bad shit is going to happen. In that situation everybody loses. You've got something Tony needs… a connection in Canada. You set him up in Canada and give him ten percent of your take here in your other businesses. He gives you some police cover and lets you run your thing your way by yourself, no interference. He then gets you preferential treatment for your construction company on job bids. Everybody wins, everybody is happy! What do you think?"

A seemingly agitated Enzo now responded in Sicilian to his son. "Do you know what that cocksucker is going to use that connection for? For drugs! Why should I jeopardize my operation for a fucking drug dealer? That's serious shit and the Feds don't look the other way on that, especially when it becomes an international thing. Besides, my people might get nervous and not want to do business with me anymore. It's out of the question."

Alex thought a bit and countered. "Don't use the same pipeline, get the guys in Canada to establish a different one. They can find the right people and then just turn it over to Tony's people. You and your people don't need to have anything to do with it. Dad, things could get ugly if you don't broker a deal with Tony. Then what? Lose everything anyhow?"

Enzo was silent for a moment walked to the other end of the workshop and sat down in his chair. He lit a cigar, blew a few puffs of smoke, looked at Alex and asked him a question. "Gabriella, you like her, don't you? Hmmmmm! You talk to Tony about this yet?" Alex shook his head no. "Then how you know if he likes this idea?" Enzo asked.

"I think he'll go for it, he likes me," Alex replied.

Enzo took a big puff of his cigar, turned to his son and responded in Sicilian.

"You think he is still going to like you when he finds out you are fucking his daughter?"

Alex took a deep breath. "Leave her out of this. Do I talk to him or not?" an angry Alex asked.

"*Do whata da fuck you wanna do*," shouted Enzo as he left the room.

Alex knew his father was not happy with what he had to do to keep the peace. Deep down inside Enzo knew that he had no other choice in the matter. A war certainly would be in no one's best interest and, while he realized that Alex had the best interest of the family in mind, he was hesitant to allow Alex to get involved in his affairs. Still, he was willing to give Alex a chance at brokering an agreement with Tony. While uneasy about it, he felt a sense of pride in his son's actions.

Alex went back upstairs and sat next to Gabriella in the sunroom. Enzo entered the room and sat next to Louise. Louise turned to Enzo, smiled and said, "They make a nice couple don't you think?

"Beautiful, very nice. Let's go to bed and *leava da kids* alone," Enzo replied.

"Good night," Gabriella said to Enzo and Louise.

Louise went over to Gabriella hugged her and whispered in her ear,

"*Bella.*" A short while later Alex took Gabriella back home.

Alex escorted Gabriella to her front door and kissed her goodnight. As he was driving down the street away from her house he noticed Tony coming down the street. He flashed his high beam headlights and Tony stopped along side his car. Alex asked him to meet him for breakfast the next morning. Tony agreed. They would meet at the Your Host Restaurant in the West Side Plaza the next day at 8 a.m.

Alex had the whole night to think about how he would approach Tony the next day. He felt confident he could finally put this agreement to bed.

The next day Alex put the proposition in front of Tony at breakfast. Tony smiled, patted Alex on the cheek and said, "Good kid, I like you. Done deal. Tell your old man we'll work out the details after the holidays."

Alex left the restaurant and headed to work. He stopped at the payphone at the end of the shopping plaza to call his father and give him the good news. Alex was quite proud of his accomplishment. He cranked up his radio and sang along to some oldies as he headed to work.

The Christmas holiday came and went and Gabriella was rarely seen without her ruby pendant. It was her lifeline to Alex, it seemed. In the months that followed, Tony came to realize that Gabriella was no longer a little girl, but a young woman. He was grateful to Alex for having helped transform his daughter from a shy, somewhat reclusive girl, to a poised and positive young woman.

Alex was the true romantic, bringing her flowers and cards on every occasion. He would sing her a song every night on the telephone before she went to sleep and awaken her with a song every morning. When they made love she felt a tremendous sense of oneness with Alex. He would often remark to her that they melted into one person when they were together, sexually. She knew every moment of every day how much Alex loved her. It seemed that not a moment went by without her thinking about Alex and he would call her several times a day to remind her how much he loved her. She was confident she had found her soul mate. The relationship had grown perfect in every way.

At the end of the spring semester, Gabriella had invited several of her friends over for a backyard pool party. It was a girl's only affair, so Alex decided he would go fishing with some of his friends. Catalina had gone over early to help prepare some of the snacks for the party and was a big help to Gabriella. Catalina knew how much Alex loved Gabriella and had, herself, become good friends with Gabriella. The girls had all assembled poolside and were all swimming and having a good time. Gabriella was so busy tending to her guests that she had not even gotten into the water yet. Catalina who had been lounging poolside yelled out to Gabriella, "Gabriella, get in the water. I'll take care of the snacks."

"You sure?" Gabriella asked.

"Yeah, go ahead," Catalina replied.

Gabriella walked towards the diving board at the deep end of the pool.

Catalina noticed Gabriella was still wearing the ruby pendant that Alex had given her. "Hey sweetie. You might want to take that off before you dive in," Catalina yelled across the pool to her friend. Gabriella promptly removed the pendant and put it under the diving board for safekeeping.

Late that afternoon, thunderstorms had pushed into the area and Gabriella's guests headed for cover inside the house. As the evening darkness set in, the guests headed back to their homes. Catalina remained behind and helped Gabriella clean up. She was ready to go upstairs to take a shower before going home when the phone rang and Gabriella answered it. It seemed as though the call lasted only thirty seconds. Gabriella seemed a bit shook up after getting off the phone. As she hung up the phone she turned to Catalina and said, "Shit, I forgot my pendant outside."

"Who was that? What's wrong?" Catalina asked.

"Take your shower, I'll tell you about it when you come down. Be right in," she said to Catalina. Catalina headed upstairs to shower while Gabriella headed to the pool.

It was dark outside and to make things worse the storm had knocked out the power to the neighborhood. It was pouring down rain and thundering loudly as Gabriella approached the pool. She went directly to the diving board to retrieve the pendant she had placed underneath it. As she scooped the pendant up in her hand she was seemingly spooked by something she saw in the corner of the yard. She began to run back towards the house when she slipped, hitting her head on the diving board. She fell backwards into the pool still clutching her pendant. She struggled to keep consciousness but felt a numbness come over her body. Her mind was filled with a million thoughts as she slid into darkness. Her last ones were of her beloved Alex. Gabriella had left this world clutching her lifeline to Alex.

Alex returned from his fishing outing and headed directly home to shower and change. He had planned on spending the night at Gabriella's since Tony was not at home. As he entered the front door he heard Catalina crying in the kitchen. Nunzio approached him, put his arm around him and said to him, "I'm afraid I have some bad news."

FIFTEEN

Several years had passed since Gabriella's death. Alex was so stunned by her death that it was several months before he would even get out with his friends and do anything on a social level. He seldom discussed the tragedy with anyone. For several months after her death he visited Tony regularly, but then decided that he needed to distance himself if he was ever to move on.

He managed to stay focused on his studies, achieving good grades, despite the rigorous course load. He was determined to get through medical school.

The fall approached and Enzo suggested a weekend hunting trip with his sons to the family cabin in rural Angola. After some prompting, Alex agreed to join Nunzio and Enzo. It would be great, a guy's only weekend.

The hunting was very good with each of them bagging several grouse and rabbits.

The men took turns preparing meals using the wild game as the main course for each meal. At times it seemed as though they tried to outdo each other in their food preparation. They played cards and told stories, often times laughing until they almost cried.

It was just what Alex needed. In the weeks and months that followed, there seemed to be a change in his demeanor. He was finally enjoying life again, laughing, smiling and being one of the guys. The change was noticeable to those around him. Many of his friends would say to him "it's good to have the old Alex back again." The one facet of his life Alex had not dealt with was dating again. He had no interest in getting involved in another relationship. Stefano would invite him out to "hang out with the bitches," as he would say, but Alex always declined, saying he was too busy with schoolwork.

Gabriella was the only woman he had ever loved and her memory lingered with him. Despite the fact that several women were interested in him, he was not ready to give his heart to anyone else. The pain of losing Gabriella was still present and real.

Stefano had decided to throw a New Year's Eve party at his house that year. He asked Nunzio and Alex to help him plan it. Both agreed. Alex would handle the food arrangements while Nunzio handled the beverages. Stefano took charge of the entertainment. Stefano would see to it that everyone would have a good time.

New Year's Eve arrived and the party was going great. Everyone was having a wonderful time and, as is the case at any Italian gathering, there was no shortage of food. The house was packed with holiday revelers, including several people in the business. Enzo had made an appearance early and then headed back home. Tony Riccio had arrived early, as well, but had no intention of leaving, as he seemed to be enjoying himself immensely. Other than for an casual exchange of hellos upon his arrival, he had not spoken to Alex.

It was not as cold as usual for the time of year and Alex had managed to slip outside to the patio area to smoke a cigar. He was leaning over a railing, watching some of the guests in the hot tub at the lower end of the terrace when Tony approached him.

"Great party isn't it, kid?" Tony said to him.

"It's great, everyone seems to be having a good time," replied Alex.

"Everybody but you," Tony said to Alex.

"What's that supposed to mean?" asked Alex.

Tony put his arm on Alex's shoulder and looked down to the hot tub with him. After a few seconds he spoke to Alex. "You have to let her go, Alex. This party has more pussy than a cat convention and you're out here all alone. I know you loved her. I loved her, too. I knew my kid well; she would want you to move on. She wasn't selfish. She wanted you to be happy, too."

"It's not that easy, Tony," Alex replied, walking away.

Tony replied. "I know it's not, but if you don't make the effort it will never happen. You're a good kid, you've got a lot going for you, don't cut yourself short."

Alex walked towards Tony, put his arms around him and hugged him. "Thanks Tony, that means a lot to me." Tony walked away and went back inside to warmer surroundings. Alex soon followed.

After several glasses of wine, Alex went back outdoors to the patio to finish the cigar he had started smoking earlier. Looking down to the hot tub, he noticed that it was now free of any occupants. He decided this would be a good time for him to soak and relax. He went inside to find something to wear.

"Hey, Unc, you got some shorts for me. I want to soak in that hot tub," he said to Stefano.

"In my dresser, second drawer on the right. Help yourself," Stefano replied.

Alex changed into the shorts and headed to the hot tub. As he walked by Nunzio, his brother stopped him.

"How much wine have you had to drink, Alex?" Nunzio asked.

"Couple of glasses," Alex replied as he headed to the hot tub. Alex exited the door and slipped into the hot tub.

"He shouldn't be out there in the tub alone, he doesn't hold his liquor well," Nunzio said to Stefano who had stopped to listen to Nunzio's questioning. "I don't want him drowning out there."

One of the ladies who had been in the hot tub earlier volunteered to keep an eye on Alex.

"I haven't changed out of my swimsuit yet. I'll go out there and sit in the tub with him," she said. She exited the door and went to sit in the hot tub with Alex.

"Hi there, you're Stefano's nephew, right?" she asked. "I'm Sandra."

"That's me," said Alex. Over the next thirty minutes the two conversed about various subjects. Alex seemed relaxed and was a bit drunk. Before long, Sandra had convinced Alex to let her give him a neck and shoulder massage.

Nunzio had gone out to the patio to smoke a cigarette and to check on his brother. He could see from his vantage point on the patio that Alex was very much enjoying his massage. A few minutes later Nunzio noticed Sandra slipping down into the water with her head in Alex's lap. While Alex who was sitting with his back to him obstructed his view, it wasn't difficult to figure out what Sandra was doing. Judging from his body language, Alex was thoroughly enjoying it.

Nunzio went back inside and spoke to Stefano. "Great party man, you outdid yourself this time. It's getting late and I need to get out of here. Do me a favor. When Alex is done getting his pipe polished, get him in here and don't let him drive home. He's had a little too much to drink."

Stefano replied as he laughed. "No shit, the clam has finally come out of its shell, huh. Who is down there with him?" he asked.

"Some chick with big jugs, she was in the tub earlier," Nunzio replied.

"I'll see if I can get me a hummer when she's done with him," Stefano replied.

"Unc, get my brother in here first so he doesn't drown," said Nunzio. The two men hugged as Nunzio left the party.

Stefano went outside to the patio and noticed Sandra walking from the hot tub area towards the house. Alex was still sitting in the tub in an almost paralyzed state. When she reached the patio where Stefano was standing, he stopped her. "You must be cold, your towel is all wet," he said to her. "Why don't you go upstairs to my room and take a hot shower. Make yourself at home up there. I'll come up in a little while with some chocolate dipped strawberries and some champagne."

She replied, "I love strawberries. Can I get a shirt or something to wear out of your closet?"

"Sure sweetheart, help yourself," Stefano replied.

Sandra headed to Stefano's room as he headed to the hot tub. He knelt alongside the tub and spoke to Alex.

"You okay, man?" he asked.

"Oh yeah," replied Alex.

"Come on, get out of there," said Stefano. "I promised your brother I would get you to bed. You are going to stay here tonight, okay."

"Okay, Unc," Alex replied.

Stefano helped Alex out of the hot tub and led him to the guest room. "Get those wet shorts off and get in bed, man. I got some hot snatch waiting for me," he said to Alex.

As soon as Alex was settled, Stefano headed to his room to frolic with his chamber mate.

His last remaining guests left about thirty minutes later amidst the pounding noises and loud moans coming from Stefano's room.

Later that month, Alex had convinced Enzo that it was time to invest some money in the financial markets. Alex had scheduled a meeting with a local brokerage firm to discuss some investment options. When they arrived at the brokerage firm, they were assigned to Miss Joelle Hanson, a well-dressed, attractive investment advisor. After a two-hour meeting, some investment options were decided upon. Enzo had neglected to bring his checkbook along, so the investment transactions could not be completed. Since Enzo was not available the next day, Alex volunteered to deliver the check to the broker for him.

The next day Alex arrived at the brokerage office about thirty minutes early with check in hand. He was escorted to Miss Hanson's office and was politely asked to wait while Miss Hanson wrapped up a previous meeting. After a short wait, Miss Hanson entered the room, shook Alex's hand and greeted him.

"Sorry to keep you waiting, Mr. Melina," she said to him.

"Not to worry and please call me Alex," he replied.

"Okay, Alex," she responded. She paused, smiled at him and said. "You may not remember me, but I was at a party with you a few weeks ago.

"You were," replied Alex.

She smiled again and said, " Let me rephrase that. I was at the same party as you a few weeks ago. I wasn't with you, but I was at the party."

"The New Year's Eve party?" asked Alex.

"Yes," replied Miss Hanson.

"Small world, isn't it?" said Alex. "Who were you there with?" he asked.

She quickly replied, "My brother, Neil, Neil Hanson. He's an engineer."

"I see," he replied. "I was there with my brother, too."

She put a pen to her lips, looked at Alex and said laughing, "That didn't look like your brother in the hot tub."

Alex was speechless for a moment. " Ohhhhh, what did you see in the hot tub?"

"Let's just say enough," she replied.

Alex seemingly embarrassed replied, "For the record, I was a little drunk. Please don't judge me on that."

"I'm sorry, I am way out of line. Please forgive me," she said to Alex.

"Let's get down to business here, finish what you came here for."

Alex handed her Enzo's check. She initialed some papers, went to the copier to make copies and returned.

"Here are Mr. Melina's copies," she said. "Be sure and thank him for me. Let him know how much we appreciate his business."

Alex stood up, shook her hand and turned toward the door. He turned back and faced her once again. "Miss Hanson, I've got an idea. I need to learn more about investing. I should schedule some time with you, myself."

She replied, "Great, I've got several openings tomorrow. What time are you available?"

"I'm not," he replied, "but I am available for dinner tonight." She looked at him and said nothing. "See, while I am learning about investing, you can find out that I am really not like the guy you saw at the party."

She smiled and replied, "Okay." She took a deep breath. "Consider it a chance to redeem yourself."

"Great," Alex replied. "I'll pick you up at six." He turned and headed toward the door.

"Alex," she shouted. He stopped and turned back toward her. "Don't you want to know where to pick me up at?"

"Oh, yeah," he said. She wrote her address and phone number on a piece of paper and handed it to him.

"Great, see you at seven," he replied.

She laughed. "Are you nervous?" she asked.

"I guess I am, Miss Hanson," he replied.

She asked him, "Is it six or seven?"

"Oh six, yeah, six," he replied.

"And please call me Joelle," she said to him.

"Okay, Joelle, see you at six," he said.

That evening Alex and Joelle shared an enjoyable evening together. Alex did learn a little bit about investing and learned more about Joelle. She took the time to learn more about him, as well. There seemed to be a chemistry between them, mostly fueled by each other's eagerness to learn about the other's profession. They dated several more times over the course of the next few months and enjoyed being in each other's company.

While he had not totally forgotten Gabriella, he enjoyed being with Joelle. She was falling in love with Alex and soon began to bring up the subject of marriage. With Joelle's earning potential, Alex would not have much to worry about, financially, while going through medical school. He was not totally convinced that he loved her, but did feel good when he was with her. Feeling she was his best option, he asked her to marry him. They married and had two children together within three years.

Joelle was very supportive of Alex while he was in medical school. She managed to keep her job even after her children were born. She balanced her career, her children and her husband. Alex had only his studies to worry about, as Joelle was well in charge at home. Her true devotion was to her children. She was never away from them unless she was at work. She had even convinced her employer to allow her to work at home two days a week so she could spend more time with her children. Because of Alex's long hours away from home, she often played the role of daddy, as well. Still she never complained, taking each day in stride.

Alex was finding himself advising his father on family business matters more often. Enzo would rely on Alex for advice on finance-related matters. He would rely on Nunzio for advice on his development company projects and on street-related issues. He felt comfortable relying on his sons for advice because they were well educated and levelheaded. He felt they had a new world attitude towards his business, able to separate themselves from the old world way of doing things. While he did not want them to ever forget their cultural roots, he realized that things had to be done differently in the new world. His business flourished and conflict was kept to a minimum. Whatever conflict did arise was usually settled in a peaceful manner, unlike the old mafia dons who relied on killing people to resolve issues.

Enzo was different. He avoided resorting to violence and killing in order to run his business. He had, in Nunzio and Alex, two skilled negotiators and allowed them to mediate and settle disputes. Enzo's style of doing business kept his organization under the radar. He had strong ties to local law enforcement officials and judges and was allowed to operate his enterprise without interference. He stayed low enough to not attract attention and keep the Feds away. His success was based on staying small enough to only have to deal at a local level. He had no desire to expand his business beyond his current parameters, feeling it would jeopardize his existing business. He had a good relationship with leaders in other cities and they, too, understood that Enzo was content in controlling only his local operation. In this manner he avoided any potential turf wars with the other leaders.

SIXTEEN

Nunzio had fine-tuned the marketplace for hijacked merchandise so well that trailer loads of stolen goods were placed with buyers within forty-eight hours after being heisted. Buyers up to five hundred miles away were ready to accept trailer-loads of merchandise through the distribution system Nunzio had established. The system was so effective, that buyers often times placed orders in advance for desired merchandise. Nunzio saw to it that they paid in advance, as well. He also had the luxury of getting prospective buyers to bid on merchandise that was in short supply.

On one particular take that was supposed to contain a trailer load of power tools, it was discovered that it contained some rather unwanted merchandise instead. It seemed that by some lack of communication, this trailer also contained a small cache of H destined for Tony's narcotics network. The handlers called Nunzio to let him know what was found. Nunzio placed a call to Tony to explain what had happened. Tony quickly made arrangements to have the H separated from the rest of the cargo and picked up to continue its journey to the buyers that awaited it. As the rest of the load was taken off the trailer, several boxes containing video equipment were found. Once again the handlers called Nunzio to alert him as to their find. Nunzio instructed them to bring the equipment to the office for inspection. When the boxes were delivered, Nunzio, Stefano, Alex and Raul were present.

Nunzio opened the boxes and inspected the equipment. He turned to the others and said, "Looks like fuckin' professional video equipment. Do we have any buyers for this kind of shit?"

Stefano replied, "You can make a movie."

Alex laughed.

"Yeah a fuck movie," Nunzio blurted out. Everybody laughed. Nunzio paused for a moment and then said to the others. "Why not?" All we need is a fucker and a fuckee, we can make our own porno shit and sell them."

"He's got a point. Good idea, Nunzio," Raul said. "Men love that shit, you know."

Alex now chimed in. "We can use our networks from the bookie guys to the hijackers to peddle the stuff. It's worth a shot."

Nunzio turned to Stefano. "Get some of them slut puppies of yours to come over this week, give them a hundred dollars each and tell them their gonna be fuckin' movie queens. I don't think we'll have a shortage of men to be in the movies," he said. Bring that bitch with the big tits and big lips. You know, the one who sucked the life out of Alex on New Year's Eve."

"We get that guy who works for you that used to be the camera guy for channel 7, what's his name?" Raul asked.

Alex replied. "Oh yeah, that Freddie guy, I know who you're talking about."

This is going to be some good shit. I wanna be in one of the movies," Stefano said.

"Forget about it your dick is too small," Nunzio shouted back. They all laughed.

"Hey Raul, go get this set up quickly. This could be a moneymaker."

"We should pay the girls a bonus based on how well their particular movies sell," Alex said.

Stefano, shaking his head now, said, "Hey Alex, you need to exercise the little head sometimes too, you know." Turning to the group, he said, "Money that's all this guy thinks about, fuckin' money. We are gonna be surrounded by all this pussy and all he thinks about is paying some bitches a bonus." Grabbing his crotch he looked at Alex and said, "I got your bonus right here." Alex laughed and walked away.

Nunzio decided to let Joe Natale organize their newfound business venture. Joe was an old friend from the neighborhood who had been busted on several occasions for shoplifting. He especially liked to lift porno magazines like Hustler and Penthouse from local drug and grocery stores. He would then try to sell them on the street for less than retail value. Joe, while not a very attractive man, somehow had a way with the ladies. He was seldom seen with the same girl twice. Nunzio suggested to him that he bring in Freddie Rice who worked for Enzo's construction company. Freddie had been a camera technician for a local news channel and had lost his job due to some alcohol-related attendance issues. Enzo gave him a break, hired him and got him back on track He would be perfect for the videotaping.

Within a week, Natale had set up the entire operation. He had converted the basement in his grandmother's house to a mini production studio. In one corner of the basement was a well-furnished waiting room area to make any visitors to the facility feel welcome. Another room contained the necessary equipment to review and edit tapes. The main room was the "action room," where the videotaping took place. The room resembled a luxury suite in a five star hotel, very well appointed and decorated to a tee. Most of the furnishings were acquired through the hijacking network. Natale also had a small private office with a wet bar so he could unwind while at work.

Two months later, the video sales were bringing in thousands of dollars a week. Nunzio saw to it that everybody involved in the video operation shared in the bounty. Taking Alex's advice, he paid the girls bonuses based on how well their individual videos sold. Alex felt that paying the girls a bonus would inspire them to put their heart and soul into the taping. Nunzio had used his stolen goods network to distribute the videos and was selling videos in over ten states. The results surprised everyone, even Nunzio. What started quite accidentally as a joke had become a viable business venture.

Enzo was extremely pleased with the income that was being generated and bragged up Nunzio's accomplishment to his associates. "Pretty soon we sell the videos from New York to California, It will be more money than the gambling business." He would often times give out videos as gifts to his friends. "If you know any beautiful girls *wanna be the* movie star, tell them to call Nunzio," he would tell his friends.

Natale had a habit of demanding sexual favors from the girls he would place in his videos. He was also known to get a bit rough at times with some of the girls. Most of the time a good blowjob would do the trick for him, but other times it was weird and kinky stuff that would fill his need. Nunzio had received several complaints from various people about Natale's behavior, but chose not to intervene. What he was not aware of was that Natale had a drug problem that was getting gradually worse.

Most of the movies up to this point in time had been of heterosexual lovemaking or provocative females stripping and dancing. Natale had decided to spice things up a bit and began to shoot lesbian love scenes to add to the collection. From there he moved on to females masturbating and using sex props such as dildos and vibrators. These videos became an instant hit. Sales of the videos increased twofold.

He would often times invite his friends to the studio to watch the tapings and would boastfully yell out instructions to the girls to show off in front of his friends. He would yell out things like "Come on baby spread them farther" or "Let me hear you moan, you fuckin' bitch." The girls were always accommodating to his requests and this made him feel powerful. He would then turn to his friends and say to them, "You see how they listen to me, man. These fuckin' bitches love me!"

During one taping session where several of his friends were present, Natale got overly involved in the taping. He had arrived at the studio strung out on drugs and was exhibiting aggressive and, at times, obnoxious behavior. Raul who was present also, was tempted to ask him what he was on, but thought better of it.

The scene that was being shot required the actress to masturbate using a large dildo. Not pleased with the performance, Natale yelled out to the actress, "Hey, honey, get into it more, look more alive, like your enjoying it."

The crew stopped taping and started shooting the scene over again. Once again Natale stepped in. He ran into the room saying, "Listen, you fuckin' whore, I said get into it! Nobody wants to see some bitch playing with herself and not enjoying it!"

The young actress replied, "I'm trying, I'm trying. What the hell do you want from me?"

Natale replied in an erratic manner. "What do I want? Let me show you goddamit! Lay back, spread them legs."

The actress complied with his request. Natale took the dildo into his right hand and began to steadily rub the dildo onto her clitoris. She began to moan loudly, "See that's how you do it," he said to her. He began to laugh wildly. "Oooh, you like that," he said to her as she began to moan louder while he rubbed faster and harder. He now turned to the group that was watching and asked them, "Any of you guys ever see a cunt this big?" He laughed even louder. Suddenly he rammed the entire dildo into the young girls vagina. "Take the whole thing, you fuckin' cunt, and next time listen the first time, bitch!" he yelled to the actress. As she screamed in pain, Natale slapped her across the face twice, gashing her upper lip.

He laughed wildly and continued to taunt her even as she lay in pain. She was now bleeding profusely from her vagina. She rolled off the bed and onto the floor, bent over in pain. Natale walked over to her and began to unbutton his pants. "Give me a blow job before you go home to mama," he taunted her.

Just then, Raul who had been watching Natale's erratic behavior stepped in and pulled him away. "Are you fucking crazy, *goddamm* it?" he asked him as they wrestled to the ground. A few seconds later, Freddie, the camera man, and some of the other spectators jumped in to restrain Natale who was swinging wildly and had begun to break up some of the furniture in the room.

"You fuckin' spic, I'll kill you, motherfucker," Natale screamed at Raul as the others restrained him.

Turning to the others Raul said "Get him out of here, take him home." Raul now turned his attention to the girl. "Are you okay?" he asked.

Staring at the ground she moaned, "Oh my God, oh my God." She seemed to drift in and out of consciousness.

"We need to get her to a hospital," Raul said to Freddie. Freddie agreed.

As Freddie and some of the crewmembers carried the young girl to the car, Raul got into his car and headed to Nunzio's. He still could not believe what had transpired at the studio. He knew he should have questioned Natale when he first noticed his erratic behavior. He also knew Nunzio was going to ask why he didn't. Drug use was something the Melinas forbade in their organization and Raul had long suspected that Natale was getting high. Against his better judgment, he chose to ignore his suspicion.

It took about fifteen minutes for Raul to arrive at Nunzio's house. As he pulled into the driveway he noticed Stefano's car parked there, as well. He ran up to the door and knocked on the door where Nunzio's wife greeted him. "Hey Rosie, can I talk to Nunz for a minute?" He very politely asked.

With a big smile on her face she replied, "Sure, come on in, he's in the rec room with Unc." "Thanks, Rosie," he said to her as he walked towards the rec room.

"I'll get you a cold beer, okay," she said back.

Raul yelled across the room to her, "You're a sweetheart. Someday I'll have me a woman like you."

Nunzio and Stefano looked towards the door as they heard Raul approaching.

"You working late tonight Raul?" asked Nunzio.

Raul replied. "I gotta talk to you guys. Some bad shit happened at the studio."

Stefano who had been standing by the foosball table with a cigar in his mouth walked towards Raul. Nunzio suddenly had a concerned look on his face. "What kind of shit?" asked Stefano.

Just then, Rosie walked in with a cold beer for Raul. "Here you go, Raul," she said to him as she handed him the beer.

"Thanks, Rosie, you're the best."

"Tell that to Nunz," she responded.

Nunzio looked at her and said, "Close the door on the way out."

She hesitated, looked at him and said, "You meant *please* close the door on the way out, didn't you?"

Nunzio replied with a sarcastic grin on his face, "Yes dear, PLEASE!!!!!!!"

"That's better," she replied as she closed the door.

Nunzio looked at Raul and said to him, "Do yourself a favor, stay single." They all laughed.

Stefano chimed in again. "So what the hell happened?"

Raul recounted the story to Stefano and Nunzio. Nunzio just shook his head.

Stefano asked, "Where is the cocksucker now?"

"The guys took him back to his place," replied Raul.

"What about the girl?" asked Nunzio.

"Freddie took her to Columbus," replied Raul.

"Raul, Alex is at home. I just talked to him. Go over there, let him know what happened and tell him to find out what he can from the hospital; see how the girl's doing. Keep us informed. Me and Unc gonna go pay this son-of-a-bitch a visit."

Raul went to Alex's house to inform him of what had taken place. After hearing the story, Alex insisted they go to the hospital.

"Alex, I don't think that's a good idea. Nunzio wants to keep a low profile," Raul said to Alex.

"You mean, don't get me mixed up in the family business, don't you? Screw that! You going with me?" Alex asked as he headed towards the door.

"Shit, I'll be lucky to have a job after all this," replied Raul. They both headed to the hospital.

Nunzio and Stefano had by now arrived at Natale's house. Before leaving, Stefano had picked up a piece of PVC pipe, about three inches in diameter and two feet long. They made their way to the front door, Stefano, with pipe in hand. Natale answered the door after about three knocks. He was in his boxers and tee shirt. "Hold your fucking horses, I'm coming," he said as he opened the door.

When he opened the door Nunzio stepped behind him and put him in a chokehold.

"You lousy piece of shit; I give you a job and this is what you do. You think we need these kinds of headaches? We're trying to stay low profile, remember?" Nunzio blurted out as Natale sank to his knees. Nunzio pushed him to the ground face down and was now pressing between Natale's shoulder blades with his knee.

Stefano reached down and tore away Natale's underwear. "I shove this pipe up your ass and you see how it feels you bastard," Stefano yelled to him. Natale squirmed so as to prevent Stefano from jamming the pipe up his rectum. After struggling for about thirty seconds, Stefano struck him over the head with the pipe several times rendering him unconscious.

"Come on Unc, let's get out of here," said Nunzio.

"Let me shove this up his ass first," replied Stefano.

"Forget it! Come on, let's go!" said Nunzio. They left, albeit Stefano a bit disappointed at not having accomplished what he had set out to do.

Meanwhile at the hospital, Alex had spoken to the emergency room doctor who told him that they would have to perform surgery to repair the girls perforated uterus. Alex asked if he could see her before they wheeled her into surgery. The doctor agreed. Alex and Raul entered the room together. Raul remained standing by the doorway as Alex sat in a chair next to her. She curiously looked up at him.

"I'm a medical student at the university and I do some of my clinical training here, but that's not what I came here to see you about. The people that you work for, the video people, I know them very well. I understand you don't have health insurance, is that right?" Alex asked her. She nodded in the affirmative. "Well, they have agreed to pay all your medical expenses and they are going to give you a few bucks to hold you over when you get out of here."

Raul's eyes bulged from his head as he raised his eyebrows.

Alex continued. "As for the man who did this to you, I don't think you will ever have to worry about him again."

Tears filled her eyes as she whispered, "Thank you," to Alex.

He responded, "The people at this hospital are really good. They will take good care of you." He smiled as they exited the room.

As they headed back to the car, Raul asked, "Nunzio says it's okay to pay the bills?"

Alex replied, "I think it's the right thing to do, don't you? I'll tell my brother and my father, too. We have an obligation here."

Raul replied jokingly, "I think I really gonna lose my job! Holy monkey shit."

"Yeah, holy monkey shit, Raul, holy monkey shit is right," Alex replied. Both laughed as they got into the car.

SEVENTEEN

Holidays were special times at the Melinas. The entire family would gather on Christmas Eve and exchange gifts. The Christmas Eve festivities were usually held at Enzo's house. The women would gather in the kitchen and roast Italian sausages and pan fry pork cutlets. Enzo would order sausage buns from Balistieri's Bakery and cheeses from Salerno's Deli to serve with the sausages and pork cutlets. *Cardoons* (burdock stalks) picked in the summer and frozen until now, were breaded, fried and sprinkled with grated cheese. Cannoli's from Costanzo's bakery were served for the dessert course of the meal.

The eating would start at about 9 p.m. and last until about 11 p.m. There were usually about thirty family members present as all of Raimondo's and Anna's children, grandchildren and great-grandchildren would be present. At precisely midnight, every family member would hug and kiss each other on the cheek and the exchange of presents would begin.

Raimondo and Anna usually hosted the Christmas Day festivities. Once again the woman would gather in the kitchen to prepare the day's meal. The meal usually consisted of baked pasta with tomato sauce and cheese, turkey stuffed with ground pork and beef and a large serving of Anna's meatballs. Food was always in abundance and Enzo was proud to have his homemade wine accompany the meal.

Raimondo would spend his time on this day telling stories about the old country to Alex, Nunzio and Catalina. Since he spoke no English, he would ask them to translate his stories to their children. He would hand out Stella Dora cookies to the great-grandchildren who were best behaved. The years had mellowed Raimondo. A delicate heart condition limited his activities. He spent his day reading an Italian language newspaper that Stefano had arranged to have delivered to a local newsstand where Stefano would pick it up. He enjoyed having his entire family together for holidays immensely and looked forward to it every year.

It was very obvious to everyone on this particular holiday that Enzo and Louise had reached a low point in their relationship. There was little verbal communication between the two of them at the gathering. The gifts they had presented to each other were purchased without any feeling or meaning. It was a meaningless, sterile exchange. With all of her children now grown, Louise was ready to end her marriage to Enzo.

In March of that year, Louise had informed Enzo that she was leaving. He vehemently objected and threatened her with bodily harm. He swore that she would not leave the country alive. Fearing for her life, she fled the country, returning to Belgium by way of Canada. Louise had avoided Enzo's henchman by arranging a car ride to Montreal under the cover of darkness. Enzo's men were positioned to intercept her at the Toronto International Airport the next day where her flight to Belgium originated. She wisely chose to drive to Montreal to connect with her flight at its stopover point there. She had outsmarted Enzo and eluded her pursuers.

While Nunzio, Alex and Catalina were not pleased with Louise's decision to leave, they understood her reasons and were sympathetic towards her. Raimondo and Anna were devastated by the news. Never before in the Melina family history had there been a divorce. Later that spring, Enzo sent Alex to Belgium to plead for his mother's return. Ten days later, Alex returned with the news, she was not coming back.

Enzo had made arrangements with his attorneys to file for divorce on grounds of abandonment. The attorneys petitioned the court to not allow Louise any claims to property, cash or investments based on these grounds. Since the local judge who was hearing the case was on Enzo's payroll, it was ruled that Louise was entitled to nothing but the clothing in her closet. Louise had gone from having it all to having nothing.

Enzo carried on with his life and stayed immersed in his business. After only a few months he began to date other women. He would often call his sons afterwards to fill them in on his experiences.

One evening, Enzo had taken one of his dates to a movie theater. After exiting the movie theater, he got into his car and drove away and headed to a local restaurant. He noticed a car parked across the way that had followed him out of the parking lot. He watched in his rearview mirror as the car followed him to the restaurant. The car had parked down the street and Enzo could see that there were two men inside.

Upon his arrival at the restaurant, he phoned Nunzio to inform him of what was taking place. Fearing that this could be a set up for a hit, Nunzio arranged to have Enzo snuck out of a back door into a van and driven away. Raul Acosta then approached the suspicious vehicle from behind. As he got closer he noticed the license plates, *U.S. GOVERNMENT*. He quickly turned around and headed in the opposite direction. He drove back to Nunzio's where Enzo had been taken. He hastily went inside to deliver the news.

"Bad news, boss," he said. "It's Federal guys."

"Oh shit," Nunzio said. "You talk to them?" he asked.

"No, I see the plates. I did not go near then," Raul replied.

"Good, good, you did the right thing, Raul," Nunzio said.

"What the Feds want with us?" asked Enzo.

"Don't know, Dad. Let's get everybody to lay low until we know what's going on," replied Nunzio. "We'll send some guys back to get your car, you should probably spend the night here until we figure out what these pricks are up to."

"If the woman is still at the restaurant somebody give her a ride home," Enzo said. "I told her I was going to the bathroom when I left the table."

Nunzio laughed. "She probably thinks you fell in," he said.

"It's no a big deal if she left, she told me she doesn't want to have sex. Why do I want to buy dinner for a woman who is not going to have sex? It's cheaper to make a sandwich at home," Enzo said.

Nunzio turned to Raul and said, "Get someone over to the restaurant to get his car. If the woman is still there, give her a ride home."

"Okay, boss, what she looks like?" asked Raul.

Enzo replied, "Nice looking redhead, she's got a green dress and big white earrings."

"What the fuck you do, take out a Christmas tree?" asked Nunzio.

"I go, boss, I go get the car," said Raul. "You want I should tie the Christmas tree to the roof of the car?"

"Looks like two damn comedians here tonight," responded Enzo. "Just go."

Raul went back to the restaurant and drove Enzo's car back to Nunzio's place. By the time he arrived back at the restaurant the G-Men were no longer there.

Enzo and Nunzio went to bed that night wondering what reason Federal Agents could possibly have to follow Enzo. Their local law enforcement friends had not alerted them to any federal investigations that might be going on. Both men spent a restless night knowing that the Feds may have come to play in their back yard.

The next day, Nunzio made several inquiries with his local law enforcement contacts, but turned up nothing. They had received no indication that the Feds were stepping up the heat on the local mobs. While business went on as usual, everyone was now looking over their shoulders, paying close attention to anything unusual.

That weekend, Alex and Joelle attended a surprise birthday party for her aunt's fiftieth birthday. Joelle had not seen her aunt and uncle in several years, but felt obligated to attend this momentous occasion. Upon arrival, Joelle introduced Alex to members of her family that he had not previously met. Uncle Nick, Joelle's father's brother, shook Alex's hand vigorously at their introduction.

"Good to meet you, Alex," he said. "I understand your going to be a doctor, maybe we can hook up and talk later."

Alex replied. "That's fine, good to meet you also, sir."

Some time had passed at the party. Alex was admiring Joelle's Uncle Nick's wildlife trophy head collection in his game room when he entered the room.

"I bagged all of them myself," he said to Alex.

"You must hunt all over the country," replied Alex.

"I do. That ram head came from the mountains out west," Nick said.

"What do you do for a living?" asked Alex.

"I'm with the FBI," replied Nick.

Alex remained silent for a moment. "Been there long?" he asked.

Nick replied. "Twenty-seven years. Went there right out of college."

Alex remained silent.

"I'm glad to see that you have chosen to become a doctor and not go into your old man's business," Nick said to him.

Alex quickly replied. "I'm not the gritty construction type. I'm not too mechanically inclined. I enjoy medicine."

Nick hesitated for a moment and smiled. "Listen, kid, you don't have to bullshit me. I know what your old man does for a living. Him and Riccio control the fuckin' mob in this town. Don't insult me by playing stupid."

Alex was insulted, but said nothing in response. After a few seconds he headed to the door.

"Well, sir, thank you for having us. Joelle and I need to scoot, our babysitter needs to be home early tonight," Alex said to him. He then exited the room and sought out Joelle.

"Joelle, get your coat, we need to go," Alex said to her.

"What's wrong?" she asked.

"I called home and Frankie is throwing up," he replied.

"Oh, wow. Let's go," she said. They quickly said goodbye to the other guests and left. About five minutes after leaving, Alex informed Joelle that Frankie was not ill. He filled her in on his conversation with her Uncle Nick.

"It made me quite uncomfortable," he said to her.

"You made me leave the party for that, Alex?" she responded. "You're an asshole."

"Excuse me, but I don't need to be verbally accosted like that," Alex said. "I don't need that crap from anyone."

She replied, "Oh yeah, that's right, I forgot. You mobsters don't take crap from anybody. They just turn up dead somewhere."

"You're way out of line, Joelle," he responded.

"No, Alex, you're out of line, you're whole damn family is out of line," she said to him. "How is it going to feel to your kids when they go to school and the other kids tell them their family is a bunch of gangsters?"

"They are not gangsters, they are business people and, besides, it has nothing to do with me," Alex replied.

"It has everything to do with you, Alex," she said. "You're always having to go over there to advise your father on sensitive business matters. Whenever others are around, you guys always find a private place where you can talk. What's there to hide if all this is legit? Alex, do you want to be a physician or be involved in your father's business? You can't do both."

"You know nothing about my father's business," Alex said.

"Oh, that's right, that's because you guineas have this secret code thing. Everything is a big secret unless you have Sicilian blood," she said. "Alex, I am your wife. You treat me like an outsider."

Alex drove on and remained silent. Until this point he had no idea that Joelle harbored these feelings. Alex had never discussed his father's business with her, nor had she ever inquired. He realized that although Enzo had managed to stay out of the limelight, there were still enough allegations in the media linking him to organized crime. No matter how differently Enzo handled his business, the fact was that he was still a member of the Cosa Nostra. Alex turned to his wife.

"You can't believe everything you read in the papers," he said.

"Alex, don't do that to me," she said.

"Do what to you?" he asked.

"Treat me like I'm stupid," she replied.

"All right, fine, let's just not talk about it anymore," he said.

"That's you're way of handling things, don't talk about it," she said to Alex. "Do you think if you don't deal with something it will just go away? Maybe it will, Alex. Maybe those around you will go away, too, if you keep ignoring them."

"What's that supposed to mean?" asked Alex.

"Figure it out, Alex, you're smart enough," she replied.

Alex pulled into the driveway and turned off the ignition. Both he and Joelle stared straight ahead for several seconds and said nothing. He opened the door and began to slide out of the car when she spoke. "I'm sorry I called you a guinea."

Alex said nothing in response. Both entered the house and, after paying the babysitter, Joelle headed up to their bedroom. Alex, still reeling from Joelle's comments earlier, went into the darkened living room and laid on the sofa. He felt so angry with Joelle that he did not want to be near her. Alex spent the night on the sofa and arose early the next morning.

He went to his grandparent's house for breakfast, seeking the wisdom of his grandfather's words. After breakfast he asked his grandfather to take him out to his garden to pick some of his prized zucchini and tomatoes.

After picking some of his grandfathers prized vegetables both men sat outside on a bench. Alex told his grandfather about his and Joelle's discussion the night before. His grandfather offered his words of wisdom.

"For so many years in the old village, we were the ones who were pushed around and intimidated. There was no justice other than that which a man made for himself. The Andreo's were the princes and we were the paupers. We avenged the atrocities against our family, but at what price? We were forever to be on the run. Our family went to Belgium and there we were a minority, an underclass. We learned to live with it. Then your father came here to America, he became successful. He gained power, not because he had a lust for it, but because he wanted this family to finally be free of playing the role of pauper. But holding power has a price. You have to all always look behind you. Your circle of trust becomes very small. Women, they don't understand. They can't understand. They don't know enough. We cannot tell them when we are bound by a code of silence. So it becomes a two-edged sword; break the silence and you risk your life in the future, say nothing and they draw their own conclusions."

Alex smiled as he listened attentively. "What about grandma, what does she know?" he asked.

"She knows nothing and she has never asked any questions," his grandfather said.

"But that was then and this is now. Women are different these days, the world is different. Women can make their own way in the world today. They are well-educated and curious. Your wife, she is intelligent, well-educated. She knows even when you don't tell her. She may choose to ignore it, she may not."

He stood up and sat back down closer to Alex. "Take my advice, you don't need to be involved in this thing of your father's. To tell you the truth, I don't know why he is involved in it. In Sicily it was different. It meant survival. Why does he need this? He has other successful business ventures that don't pose him any risks. You want to know why your mother left? She left because this thing is his mistress. You decide. Do you want this to be your legacy? You are his most trusted advisor; if anyone can make him change it is you. Nothing lasts forever; this thing will bring everyone down eventually. Don't loose your family, too."

His grandfather embraced him and went back inside. Alex drove away, pondering what he was told.

EIGHTEEN

Catalina had awoken at her usual time and was getting ready for work when the telephone rang. On the telephone was her friend, Ruth, who worked for the district attorney's office as a legal aide.

"Hey, Cat, it's Ruthie," she said.

"Hey, Ruthie, is everything all right?" Catalina asked.

"I need a big favor, I hope you can help," Ruth said.

"Okay, what is it?" Catalina asked.

Letting out a big sigh, Ruth continued. "My car has a flat tire and I needed to pick up some papers from a detective at Precinct Twelve to give to the DA. I told him I would be there by nine but triple A hasn't shown up yet to change my tire. You think you could swing by and get them for me on your way in?"

"Sure, but why don't I come and get you, too?" Catalina asked.

"The DA needs the papers this morning before the ten o'clock meeting, if you come here to get me you'll never get them to him on time," Ruth replied.

"All right, I'll get them and take them to the DA. I'll call you from there. If they still haven't changed your tire by then, I'll come back and get you," Catalina said.

Ruth said, "Sounds great, thanks, you're a sweetheart, girl. Ask for detective Solon when you get there."

"Talk to you later," Catalina said as she hung up the phone.

Catalina drove directly to Precinct Twelve to pick up the papers for her friend, Ruth. She approached the desk at the precinct and introduced herself.

"Hello, I'm here to see detective Solon," she said to the desk sergeant. Just then a man in a shirt and tie approached from behind the desk.

"I'm Solon, you must be Cat. Your friend called me and told me you were on your way. Thanks for coming."

"You're very welcome, sir," Catalina responded.

The detective handed her an envelope stuffed with papers. "Tell the DA this is all we got on the Millner Avenue bust. It was just some stuff we found in the car. We'll get the other evidence over to him as soon as the forensic guys are finished with it."

"Thank you again, Detective Solon," Catalina responded.

"You're welcome and I appreciate you coming out here" he responded.

Catalina took the envelope and got into her car and drove away. As she was driving, she was thinking to herself that the name Millner Avenue sounded familiar, but she could not place it. She thought to herself, "Millner, Millner, where do I know that name from?"

Suddenly it came to her. It was the street directly behind Tony Riccio's house. She now became curious. "What kind of bust happened on Millner Avenue?" she thought to herself. She finally pulled her car over to the side of the road and opened the envelope.

The envelope contained an arrest report on the man who had been arrested. She read the first few pages. His name was Luis Gonzalez, a Puerto Rican who had come to the mainland two years ago. He had some priors for assault and battery and was supposedly tied into the Loco Loco drug cartel. Undercover police followed him to a Millner Avenue home after he had sold drugs to some junkies in a schoolyard. They arrested him after observing the transaction and following him to Millner Avenue. The envelope also contained a smaller envelope which had some items seized from Gonzalez's car. On the outside of the envelope was a big question mark written in red and small lettering, listing the items had been found in his possession.

What Catalina found next was even more interesting. In the envelope was a picture. It was obviously taken from a distance. It was of a man sitting by a pool, being handed what appeared to be an envelope by another man. While the faces were not recognizable in the picture, the pool area was very familiar to Catalina. She noticed an old wagon wheel between some oak barrel flower planters in the picture; the same ones that were in Tony Riccio's pool area. It was unmistakenly the Riccio pool.

She wondered to herself, "Why would this guy have a picture of Tony's pool in his possession?" Apparently the police were not able to make out the identities of the people or the location of the photograph and had written the question mark on the envelope in reference to it.

While she wasn't one hundred percent certain, she knew somehow this had something to do with the union and Tony and quite possibly her own father. Before delivering the envelope to the district attorney, she stopped at her own office across the street and made copies of the files and photographs. She then placed her copies in her trunk and delivered the envelope to the DA.

The receptionist at the DA's office told Catalina that Ruth had called and she had gotten her tire fixed. She was on her way and did not need Catalina to pick her up.

Catalina went back to her office and tried to reach Nunzio. When she could not reach him she called Alex.

"Alex, it's me, Catalina. What are you up to?"

"Just got out of the shower, sis, everything all right?" Alex asked.

"Oh yeah, everything is fine. I stumbled across something interesting today, thought you might be interested," she replied.

"Oh yeah, like what?" Alex asked.

She whispered, "I'm at work, can't talk. Come see me later, around five, okay."

He replied, "See you at five."

Five o'clock came and Alex, prompt as ever, arrived at Enzo's. Catalina was waiting for him in her room. "Alex come up here" she said to him. "Close the door."

Catalina was sitting on the edge of her bed holding the envelope. She pulled out the arrest report and handed it to Alex. He took a moment and read it, then shrugged his shoulders.

"What, what is this?" he asked.

"There's more," she replied, handing him the photograph.

"Looks like Tony's place," said Alex, after studying the picture.

"See the address of the arrest, it's Millner Avenue, Alex. Right behind Tony's," said Catalina.

"You're kidding me," replied Alex.

"No, I'm not," she replied.

"Do you still have the key to Tony's that Gabriella gave you?" Asked Alex.

"I think so," she replied. She went to her jewelry drawer and found the key. "This is it, Tony told me to keep it in case I ever wanted to come over and use the pool."

Alex replied. "Give it to me, I need to go check something out."

"I'm going with you," Catalina said, handing him the key. They both got into Alex's car and drove to Tony's house. Alex pulled into the driveway.

"I don't think he's home," said Catalina.

"He's in Houston, I talked to him last night," said Alex. "Go in the house and turn off the alarm."

Alex went through the garage and out to the pool area. Catalina now joined him there. Holding the picture, he looked at the houses behind Tony's. "That one, that one there," Alex said pointing to a house behind Tony's. He proceeded across a small wooded area separating the two houses. Catalina followed closely behind.

"Where are you going?" she asked.

"Follow me and stay quiet," he replied. Alex walked directly towards the house behind Tony's and stopped about thirty yards short of the house. He looked back towards Tony's and then back to the other house.

"That's got to be the one," he said.

"What's that?" asked Catalina, pointing to a communication relay box in the woods.

"That's where they hook up the telephone wires for the neighborhood," replied Alex. He walked towards the box with Catalina closely behind. "All the wires are underground and come into this junction box. It handles all these houses in the neighborhood."

"Here is one they forgot to bury," Catalina said as she kicked off some leaves and exposed telephone line lying on the ground.

"*Ummm*, that's odd," said Alex. "Why is this one running into the box and to that other house along the ground? Looks like someone put that line in after everything else was hooked up. Looks suspicious to me." Alex walked around the box looking for other wires.

"Let's call Nunz and get an electrician or somebody over here to check it out, Alex," said Catalina.

"We can call from your portable phone," said Alex.

They both walked back to Tony's house and went inside. "I gotta take a leak, see if you can get Nunz on the phone," Alex said to his sister as he headed to the bathroom.

Alex was now urinating in the background as Catalina phoned Nunzio.

Catalina with the phone to her ear yelled out to Alex. "You could at least close the door."

On the other end of the phone line a voice answered.

"Close the door to what?" It was Nunzio. Catalina had not realized that he had answered the telephone.

"Sorry, Nunz, I didn't expect you to answer so fast. Me and Alex are at Tony's and your brother is in the toilet pissing and he doesn't close the door," Catalina said to Nunzio.

"Why did you guys go all the way to Tony's just to take a leak?" asked Nunzio.

"We didn't come here to take a leak, we came here to check something out," she replied. "Sorry about the poor connection, but I'm on my portable phone."

Alex walked back into the room and gestured to Catalina, "Let me talk to him." Catalina handed the phone to Alex and said, "I gotta go, too, and I hope you at least raised the toilet seat, Alex."

Alex replied, "Sis!"

Catalina turned and said, "What?"

Alex replied, "Don't forget to wipe."

Catalina shaking her head, said to her brother, "Alex, you're disgusting."

Alex now spoke into the phone, "She loves me."

"What's going on, little brother?" asked Nunzio.

"Catalina got this information on this drug bust that went down on Millner, behind Tony's house. The dude was a part of the Loco Loco gang. You know the guys Tony has problems with. Well, get this. The guy who got busted had pictures of Tony by his pool. I think they were taken from the house behind his on Millner. The fuzz don't know it's Tony cause the pictures aren't real clear, but you know the barrel planter and wagon wheel in his yard? It shows up real good," Alex said to Nunzio.

Nunzio replied. "Damn!"

"Wait, it gets better, bro," Alex said to Nunzio. "Me and sis, we took a walk in the woods between the two houses. We found an unburied telephone line from the house on Millner to the relay box in the woods. I bet they tapped into his telephone line. The line runs from the box to the house where the pictures were shot from."

"How do you know?" asked Nunzio.

"If you see the pictures, you can tell by the angle of the shot," said Alex. "It's the only house the pictures could have been shot from."

"Tony know?" asked Nunzio.

"He's in Houston," replied Alex.

"Is anybody in the other house now?" asked Nunzio. "Let's make sure before you go out there again."

Catalina now re-entered the room. "Is he sending someone over?" she asked.

Alex held up a finger asking her to wait a second.

"Nunzio, can you get someone here to check it out?" asked Alex.

Nunzio replied, "I'll be there in twenty minutes, see you soon. Stay out of sight until we know you are not being watched."

Alex hung up the phone. "What did he say?" asked Catalina.

"He's on his way," Alex replied.

"What do you think all this means, Alex?" asked Catalina.

"I'm not sure, but I think we are going to find out," replied Alex.

Catalina placed her hands over her lips. "Alex, no one can ever find out I gave you guys that stuff, okay, I could loose my job or go to jail."

"Sis, your old man is Enzo Melina, you wouldn't go to jail. Lose your job, *mmaaaybe*. Go to jail, *naaahhhhhh*," Alex said jokingly.

About thirty minutes passed and Nunzio arrived. He entered the house with some tools in hand. "Hi, guys, where is it?" he asked.

"Follow me" Alex replied. "Cat, stay here inside."

"Yes, boss," Catalina replied.

Alex and Nunzio exited the rear and walked to the woods together.

"Why is she here?" Nunzio asked Alex.

"She is the one who discovered all this, what did you want me to do?" replied Alex.

"Whatever you do, don't tell the old man she even knows about this shit okay," Nunzio said to Alex.

Alex stopped suddenly and replied. "Nunzio, stop treating us like morons or little kids, man."

"Take it easy, Alex, I'm sorry, all right," said Nunzio.

The two men began to walk again. Alex pointed towards the house. "That's the one right there." He said to his brother. "There's the green phone box."

Nunzio stood over the box observing the exposed wiring. "Let's get the cover off and see where it all goes," he said to Alex. Using his tools, he removed the cover and knelt alongside the now coverless box.

"What do you think?" asked Alex.

"These guys are slick. That's what they did, they tapped his fuckin' line. You were right," replied Nunzio. "They probably know every move he makes before he even makes it. Question is, how much do they know about our operations, what does Tony talk about?"

"Explains a lot, doesn't it?" said Alex. "They were always one step ahead of him cutting off his deals and pulling away his players. And all this done so simply, damn!"

"We've got to get someone into that house to have a look around. That should answer a lot of questions for us. I'll get someone here in the next day or two. In the meantime, stay clear of here, we don't want to arouse any suspicions."

Nunzio replaced the cover on the box and both men headed back to Tony's house.

Alex stopped in the yard by the pool. "It's a pretty eerie feeling being back here knowing she died here. It gives me the creeps sometimes," Alex said to Nunzio.

Nunzio replied. "You really did love her didn't you, Alex?"

"I'll never forget her, never forget her," replied Alex.

"Let's go inside, get Catalina and get out of here," said Nunzio.

Alex and Catalina drove off together while Nunzio drove away in his own car.

"What do you make of all this?" Catalina asked Alex.

"Don't know what to think right now, Cat, maybe we can put some other pieces together later and make some sense of it all," replied Alex.

"Is Tony in any danger?" asked Catalina.

"Sis, listen. You do the shit he does, you are always in danger. He chooses this life and he has to be aware of the consequences. That's all."

"You mean like Dad and Nunz?"

Alex pulled the car over to the side of the road. "Dad's thing is different, it's more controlled. No drugs, less risks. Tony, he wants it all. He shoots for the stars and the moon. He doesn't give a shit who lives or dies. If you get in the way he'll fuck you over big time. Not too many people care about the prostitution or the gambling or the fencing. People have a tendency to ignore that. Drugs—that's something different. When some damn *tizzun* sells some drugs to some kid in eighth grade and the kid OD's then everybody notices and it gets attention. Our people are not out there killing little kids," he said to Catalina.

"Do you think Dad has ever killed anyone, Alex?" asked Catalina.

Alex hesitated, rolled his eyes and answered. "No! Absolutely not and don't ever ask that question again."

"I worry about him and Nunz sometimes, I have dreams they both get killed in some shootout somewhere," Catalina, looking away, said to Alex.

Alex reached over and wrapped his arms around his sister. "Don't think like that, that's not going to happen, never," Alex whispered in her ear. "I love you, sis."

Catalina, with tears in her eyes, kissed Alex on the cheek and whispered back, "I love you, too, Alex."

Alex pulled his car back into traffic and headed back to Enzo's. Along the way he turned to his sister and asked, "Are you hungry?"

"Starving," she replied.

"There is this new little sausage stand near the hospital, no inside dining, but some outside tables to sit at. All the guy makes is sausage, hot dogs or burgers. Nothing fancy, but really good. You can get peppers and onions and all that good stuff with it. For like four bucks you get a sandwich, chips, a drink and a cookie," Alex said to her.

"Really," said Catalina.

"Yeah, its really good. He gets all his meat from the Zarcone Meat Market on the west side. Everything is fresh made and cooked to order. Let's go get Dad and go out there," said Alex.

"What's the name of this place?" asked Catalina.

"Luigi's Sausage Stand," replied Alex.

"I'm game, let's go," Catalina replied.

NINETEEN

As the years passed, Enzo's and Tony's business flourished. Enzo prospered in his legal, as well as his illegal, activities. He managed to maintain a low profile involving himself only in low-risk illegal activities, such as gambling, hijacking, vice and fencing. His enterprises controlled the contracts of waste haulers, concrete companies and food service supply companies, as well. He guaranteed his chosen suppliers with the majority of the business from the biggest customers in exchange for a piece of the action. Rival companies were forced out of business by his enforcers, eliminating the competition and establishing inflated base prices for services, making these ventures very lucrative.

Tony, on the other hand, was always looking for the home run, the big hit. It was whatever could make him the most money in the shortest period of time. Along with this approach came risk. He was heavily involved in narcotics, extortion and the corruption of union officials.

Tony and Enzo managed to co-exist mainly from a mutual respect for each other. Tony realized that Enzo had no intention to try and take over any of his existing operations. He simply wanted to control the activities that Tony had chosen not to pay close attention to and had crumbled in the process. Tony was agreeable at first, subscribing to Enzo's theory that there was enough grass in the pasture for two cows to graze on.

Each of the two men ran their own separate families with their own *capos*, lieutenants and *consiglieri's*. Enzo had the smaller enterprise of the two and fewer headaches. His organization was closer knit and his soldiers more loyal. Enzo was much more generous to those in his organization than was Tony to those in his. He managed to escape many of the problems that had besieged Tony through the years.

Riskier ventures, while producing more revenue, also required more capital to fund the risks. Payoffs, legal fees and everyday expenditures devoured a large percentage of revenue in Tony's organization. Several of his button men and soldiers had been arrested over the years and the implementation of the RICO legislation kept his activities in the spotlight. In spite of all this, he enjoyed being the big dog and basked in the glow of the power it brought him.

Although both men shared a friendship, Enzo avoided any real close contact with Tony, either socially or privately. "When the mansion at the top of the hill burns, I don't want its flames to burn down my little house," Enzo would say. For this reason, he kept his distance, choosing to communicate through emissaries, instead. Whenever the two men did find themselves at the same social functions together, Enzo would limit his contact with Tony to a warm greeting and brief discussion of legal business conditions.

Tony had total control of the narcotics market for several years. His import and distribution network stretched from Western New York, to Pennsylvania and into Eastern Ohio. He had remained unchallenged in his buying and selling of illicit drugs. He used import sources from the CAN-AM. pipeline to supply his distribution network.

Blacks and Hispanics primarily ran his distribution network. Tony's *capos* would buy the drugs and establish a base price for selling the narcotics to the distributors. The distributors or street people would get their profits from the street value of the drugs. The *capos* would often adjust their prices based on what price was being paid on the street for a hit. In this manner they made sure they kept the lions share of the profits for themselves. This angered the street level guys who felt they were taking all the risks and getting the smaller cut.

After some time, they began to seek out their own sources, realizing there was more money to be made if they could control the trade from port of entry to street. This did not sit well with Tony or any of his *capos*.

The black and Hispanic street peddlers now turned importer and distributor, were cutting into one of his largest sources of income. Tony's days of total control of the narcotics market were coming to an end. He soon received word that one of his distributors had refused to pay the asking price for his weekly bundle, offering less than the established price. The message from the street was clear. As one distributor put it, "Why should we pay your boss 5G for what we can buy for 2G?" Tony realized he had to act and act quickly.

He soon discovered that his competition was importing narcotics from South and Central America. The Medeillin Drug Cartel was importing drugs into the States with tremendous ease. Unlike his sources that were primarily based in Asia, most of the narcotics from the south could flow on the surface and be easily imported through Mexico. The remainder found it's way in through Florida, with what appeared to be an all-Hispanic pipeline. The cartel was well-organized and well-funded.

Tony sent instructions to his *capos*. "Send a message to the bastards in the street who are refusing to buy from you. Let them know that we are the game in town."

The next day one of the distributors refused to buy his weekly allotment. Tony's *capo* and his button man beat him with a bat and broke his jaw. Later that week, Tony's button man was found dead, shot execution style. His body was dumped in a city park. Word soon reached Tony. Furious over the killing, he called for a Saturday morning meeting of all his *capos* and associates from other cities. He invited Enzo and Nunzio but Enzo refused to attend, claiming that it had nothing to do with his business.

Later that evening, Nunzio and Alex drove to Luigi's Sausage Stand to get a bite to eat. Nunzio approached the stand and greeted Luigi.

"Hey Luigi, how's it going?"

"Hello, Mister Alex. Hello, Mister Nunzio. What I can get for you?" asked Luigi.

"Two Sausages with everything, Luigi," replied Alex.

"You *wanna somathing* to drink?" asked Luigi.

"Sprite," replied Nunzio.

"Lemonade," replied Alex.

A few minutes later Luigi served the men their sandwiches and their drinks. They sat at on one of the picnic tables alongside the stand.

While they were seated, Nunzio told Alex of Tony's invitation to the meeting and gave him details of the killing. "The old man won't go to it, he says it's got nothing to do with us," Nunzio said to Alex.

"It's got everything to do with us," Alex replied. Nunzio look puzzled.

"The drug thing, that's where the money is at brother. The people who control the drug trade pretty soon will control everything else. They'll be able to hire our people away from us and later on they'll get in on everything else."

"So what are you saying, we should be in on narcotics trafficking? You know how the old man feels about that shit," Nunzio said to Alex.

"That's not what I'm saying, Nunz. These black guys they don't give a shit if they go to jail. They don't value their own lives, let alone anyone else's. They don't give a shit how many people they kill. They're vicious and unrelenting. I think you're gonna see some big turf wars in the years to come. All these bastards are going to try to get in on the action and it's not going to be pretty," Alex said, shaking his head. "I think the good old days for La Cosa Nostra are coming to an end. When people start getting whacked the local authorities are going to have to react. Pretty soon the Feds will show up and all of a sudden the RICO thing is going to be used to get everybody off the streets. There used to be one mafia, now there are many. The Asians, the Russians, the black guys. Problem is, there is no central command and control, so things will get fucked up."

"You sound passionate about it, brother," Nunzio said to Alex.

Alex replied. "I can see it coming. We've got to start backing out of this shit now, so you don't lose all the legit stuff when the Feds come rolling in. They are going to tie everybody into one bundle and go after them all, drugs or no drugs."

"That's a lot of money to walk away from, Alex," said Nunzio.

"I've been doing a lot of thinking, reading all this stuff in the paper. It's happening in all the other cities. It's going to happen here, too, Nunzio," Alex said.

"Have you mentioned this to Dad?" asked Nunzio.

"Not yet, I wanted to convince you of it first," replied Alex.

Nunzio sat quietly eating his sandwich.

"You guys can still make a great living with the development company," Alex said. "You don't need this shit. It was damn good while it lasted. It's getting too risky now. We've been lucky, none of the top guys in jail, no bang-bang wars. It's all been pretty clean until now."

Nunzio took a sip of his drink and looked at Alex. He then said to him, "You're probably right, you're probably right. To be honest with you I keep thinking what would Rosie do with the kids if we all got busted. I think about that a lot. It's just hard to walk away from something this sweet. You're right, our luck is going to run out sooner or later."

Luigi who had come out of the stand to smoke a cigarette soon joined the men. "Cigarette?" he asked Nunzio.

"Thanks," said Nunzio accepting his offer.

"*I no gonna aska* you because you the doctor," Luigi said to Alex.

"Luigi, how is the sausage business?" asked Nunzio.

"*Itsa* good," replied Luigi. Turning to Alex, he said. "You *lika* the sandwich?"

"*Itsa* good, *itsa* good," replied Alex, gesturing with both hands. All three men laughed.

"You *buzineez itsa* good?" Asked Luigi.

"Not bad," replied Nunzio.

"Mister Tony *buzineez itsa* no so good," Luigi said to Nunzio.

Nunzio and Alex were speechless. They looked at each other and then at Luigi.

"Mister Tony who?" asked Nunzio.

"Riccio," replied Luigi.

Alex asked. "What do you know about Riccio?"

"I *cana talk wita* no trouble?" asked Luigi. He sat down next to Nunzio.

Nunzio laughed. "You're gonna have more trouble if you don't talk now."

"Every day, these people *comma* here to eat. I hear *lotsa* talking. Tony *dis anda* Tony *dat*. We *squeeza* him out, we *teacha* him good. I can hear good from the stand. I no say nothing to nobody. I no like *dat* the Puerto Rican and the *tizzun maka da* trouble for Italian people."

Alex and Nunzio soon learned from the conversation that several of the Loco Loco gang members hang out at a table behind the sausage stand. They have apparently assumed that Luigi cannot overhear their conversations or is not fluent enough in English to understand what they are speaking about. They were also surprised to learn that Luigi was fluent in Spanish, as well, having spent three years in Argentina prior to coming to the United States.

Alex now turned to Luigi and spoke. "Luigi, you want to make some extra cash?"

"What do you mean?" Luigi replied.

"You keep listening to these guys, then you tell me and Nunzio what they say. You call us on the telephone whenever you hear something. Call us right away, so you don't forget. We pay you to do that, okay?" Alex said.

"You no *haffa* to pay me. But *sooma* day if I *gatta* sick, I come to you and you no *charga*, okay," replied Luigi.

Alex replied, "Deal," as both men shook hands. Luigi went back into his stand as Alex and Nunzio finished their meal.

"Let's walk over to the hospital grounds," Alex said to Nunzio. "If we walk and talk no ears will hear."

Nunzio shook his head. "Amazing, isn't it. The sausage king spying on the Loco Loco's. Who would believe that shit?"

"So what do you think about what I said?" asked Alex.

"I think it has merit," replied Nunzio.

"When do you want to talk to the old man about it?" asked Alex.

"Soon, real soon, Alex. Let's leave Unc out of the discussion. I love the guy, but he has nothing positive he could contribute to that discussion. He would just say screw it, let's go kill them all," said Nunzio.

"I really feel in my heart it's the right thing to do now. There will be more potential to take steps backwards than steps forward. Besides it would kill Catalina if anybody got hurt or busted," said Alex.

"You going to let Tony in on what the sausage guy says?" asked Nunzio.

Alex replied. "Probably in time, but I won't reveal the source of the information. I still feel an obligation to Tony."

"Because of Gabriella?" asked Nunzio.

Alex sighed. "Yeah, I feel I owe it to her memory. She was such a gentle soul."

The men continued walking and talking. Nunzio said to Alex, "It's been a good ten or fifteen years for Dad. I guess all good things come to an end."

Alex replied, "Consider the extra earnings a bonus and tax-free, at that." Alex put his hand on his brother's shoulder. "There is one more thing I want to talk to you about. It's about me and Joelle."

"You're having another baby!" Nunzio said with excitement.

Alex's eyes now swelled with tears. "We're going to split up," he said. Nunzio stopped walking.

"What! First Mom and Dad and now you? What the hell! You have never said anything about this before. What's going on?" Nunzio shouted to his brother.

"It's just not working anymore. I don't know," Alex said as both men began to walk again.

Nunzio said in an upset tone. "It's just the pressure of med school and all that; give it more time. You will be done with your training soon, it will get better."

Alex stopped walking. "I've given it a lot of thought. We both think it's best."

Nunzio replied, "What about the kids?"

"I'm still their father. I'm still going to be there all the time for them," Alex replied.

"Damn, Alex, you just made my heart sink. I can't believe this," Nunzio said to Alex, waving his hands in the air.

"I guess I need to start looking for a place to live. I want Joelle and the kids to stay in the house. I'm going to find something close to the hospital," Alex replied.

"No way man! You come and stay with me and Rosie. You can have the whole basement. You will be comfortable there. You got family here, man," said Nunzio.

Alex replied. "Thanks, I appreciate it, but I don't want to be a burden."

"You're no burden, brother. Give it some thought," Nunzio said to Alex.

"I will, I really will," replied Alex.

"This is some bad shit happening with Tony and all. It's been years since anyone has been whacked," said Nunzio. "Used to be that it was necessary. It cleaned out the old blood, you know, got rid of the animosity that had built up through the years. Back then it was all *paesans*, now who the hell knows."

"Someone needs to go to that meeting," said Alex. "You know Riccio isn't gonna stand around and not do anything about one of his guys getting clipped. We need to know what his next move is going to be. He can get pretty wacko sometimes."

Nunzio replied, "I'll go to the meeting. We need to know."

TWENTY

Nunzio had put Raul in charge of finding out what was going on at the Millner Avenue house behind Tony's residence. Raul had several good informants in the Latin community who he could count on to get him the word on the street. The information that he sought began to trickle in slowly. Raul had also put the house on Millner Avenue on surveillance. His surveillance people reported back that in the last several days there had been several deliveries made, consisting of large boxes. The deliveries were made in a truck that had no markings. They had also reported that a large object resembling a propane tank had been delivered.

It appeared that the house was occupied by one man who made several trips to a nearby hardware store, daily, often times leaving the passage door to the garage open. He also left for lunch at around noon every day, eating at a local Mexican restaurant. In the evening, there were several visitors who would arrive and stay about thirty minutes and then leave. Raul felt that the best opportunity to get into the house undetected would be when the sole occupant of the house left for lunch. That would give him ample time to get into the house and look around. The next day, Raul waited at Tony's house hoping that he would have a chance to get into the house on Millner. Shortly after noon, Raul received word on his two-way radio that the coast was clear.

Raul, with camcorder in hand, made his way through the woods and to the house. He was hoping that the passage door was unlocked. He arrived to find the door locked. He reached into his pocket and took out his tools. Within a minute, he had the lock picked and was in the house. He went from room to room videotaping and making comments about what he saw. It took Raul less than twenty minutes to search the entire premises. He then exited and made his way back through the woods to Tony's house.

Raul had reported back to Nunzio that he had some interesting information to give him. The men agreed to meet at Nunzio's the next day to discuss what he had learned. Nunzio then called Enzo to ask him to join them. Enzo agreed and they set a meeting time of 10 a.m. the next morning.

Enzo had just hung up the phone when he heard a car pulling into the driveway. He peered out the window through the open blinds and saw it was Alex. The evening darkness had set in and Enzo turned on the exterior light at the end of the driveway for Alex. Alex came in and greeted his father. "Hi, Dad, what are you doing?" Alex asked.

"I just got off the phone with your brother," he replied.

"Anything going on?" Alex asked.

"I don't know yet," replied Enzo. "We are getting together tomorrow to discuss some information Raul has. Do you want a glass of wine? I was just getting ready to pour myself some."

"Only if it is your homemade wine," Alex replied. He then took a seat on the sofa.

Enzo went to the kitchen and poured both of them some wine. He was walking through the hallway into the living room, telling Alex that the meeting was set for 10 a.m. Suddenly, a loud blast rang out. In an instant, the living room window was blown out and glass was shattered throughout the living room. Enzo dove for cover behind his recliner in the living room while Alex quickly rolled off the sofa and onto the floor with his hands covering his head. His heart began to pound as he called out for Enzo. He could also hear the screeching tires of a car as it sped away.

"Alex, you okay?" Enzo asked.

"I'm fine, what about you?" he responded.

Enzo and Alex both stood up and brushed themselves off of the glass that had hit them after the blast. Both of their faces bore a startled and fearful look.

"Cocksuckers, dirty cocksuckers," Enzo shouted. "They try to hit me in my own house. I'll burn whoever it was that did this."

"Dad, who could have done this?" Alex asked.

"I wish I knew, Alex," he responded. "Call your brother, tell him to get some people over here right away. Tell him to bring a new fuckin' window, too." He then went to his bedroom and returned, armed with a 12-gauge shot gun. "Tell them bastards to come back now," he said.

Alex quickly called Nunzio to tell him what had just taken place. Nunzio, Raul and Stefano arrived about twenty minutes later accompanied by some gun-toting associates. Enzo, Alex, Nunzio, Stefano and Raul retreated to the basement workshop as the other men worked to cover the window opening in plastic.

"Any ideas who could have done this?" asked Nunzio.

"Your guess is as good as mine," replied Enzo.

Stefano turned to Alex and said, "You're white as a ghost, kid. You okay? Did you shit yourself?"

Enzo quickly replied, "Leave him alone, this is not the time to be joking around."

"He's white as a ghost, look at him," said Stefano.

"I didn't shit my pants," said Alex. "We could have both been killed here tonight. Am I scared? Yeah, I'm scared! You would be, too."

"I screwed up," said Enzo. "I forgot to close the damn blinds when it got dark. With the lights on in here, I became an easy target. I was careless." He shook his head. "I was careless."

"Dad, who would have expected a hit," Nunzio said. "It's been peaceful for a long time. We all have to be careful now."

"Things are changing," said Stefano.

"Since we are all here, let's get Raul to fill us in on what he has found out about the Millner Avenue thing," Nunzio said. "It might shed some light on all this."

Raul began to share with the others the information he had gathered. "I got video of the house on Millner. I shot every room. They have got a pretty sophisticated video set up there. They can spy on Tony whenever he is by his pool. They have got cameras and listening devices hidden in his pump room by the pool. They have got his phone tapped. These guys are good."

"Who is 'they'?" asked Enzo.

"The Loco Loco guys," replied Raul.

"How do you know it's not the Feds?" asked Stefano.

"We got some of the tapes," replied Raul. "I'm certain on this. Wait, there's more." He continued. "They put a big propane tank in the basement, there is no natural gas in the area. I would say they are setting up to cook up narcotics in the basement. Why else would you have that kind of equipment?"

"These guys are pretty serious about this shit, professionals," Stefano chimed in.

"So you think what happened here tonight is tied into all that?" asked Enzo. "I have nothing to do with Tony's shit."

"Word on the street is that Tony is flapping his gums how he is the boss and everybody answers to him," Raul said.

"Fuck Tony," said Stefano. "We should have taken him out a long time ago. Boss of my balls, that's what he is."

"You remember Natale, the video guy?" asked Raul. "He is working for this black drug runner called Soft Daddy. He's tied in with the Loco guys."

"How do you know all this?" asked Alex.

"The babe Natale put in the hospital, you know the one he tore her cunt out. She's a hooker now. Her pimp lets her hang out at this speakeasy club. She hears all kinds of stuff. When he gets high he runs his mouth about stuff, too," Raul said. "She hates Natale. He goes to the club a lot. He doesn't recognize her, doesn't remember who she is. She came and found me at the Your Host Restaurant and said she had some information for me. The Loco guys and Soft Daddy, they are trying to muscle Tony out."

"Let me see if I understand this now," said Enzo. "These guys, spics and niggers, are trying to muscle Tony out. They think we are all tied in here. First, they take out Tony's best distribution guy and now they try to clip me. This is not good!"

"Can you find out who called the hit?" asked Nunzio. "If you can, we can try and get a meeting; let these guys know we're not tied into the drug stuff and we are a separate family from Tony."

"I try boss," replied Raul.

"These guys aren't going to want to talk," said Alex. "They are different, you are not dealing with Sicilians or Italians here. They are not like us."

"We talk to them with a shotgun then," said Stefano.

"It's worth a try," said Enzo. "We have to set the record straight about our relationship with Tony."

"I'm telling you, they are not going to listen," said Alex.

"I think Alex is right, but I'm willing to give it a shot if we can find out who is calling the shots over there," said Nunzio. "This really sucks."

"Okay, what else you got for us Raul?" asked Stefano. Raul took a deep breath and exhaled.

"The night Tony's daughter died," said Raul before being interrupted by Alex.

"You mean Gabriella?" asked Alex.

"Yes, Gabriella," said Raul. "These guys were taping the pool party, you know, looking at the girls' tits and that. The camera they had hidden in the pump house stopped working. One of the guys snuck over after all the girls had left to try to put it back in focus. That left one guy in the house. He didn't realize the other jack-off had gone over to fix the camera. He calls Tony's house and tells his daughter that her ruby looks nice between her knockers. They were always prank calling her. She realized she had left it out at the pool so she went out to get it. The other guy had hidden in the corner when he saw her coming outside. She saw him when she leaned over to get her pendant and tried to run in the house. She slipped and hit her head. You know the rest of the story."

There was complete silence for several seconds. Nunzio finally broke the silence.

"Do we know these guys' names?" he asked.

"We working on it, boss," replied Raul.

Alex walked to the other side of the room. "I want these fuckers dead," he said. "They have to pay for what they did."

Enzo walked over to his son and put his arm on his shoulder. "We are in the middle of a crisis here," he said to Alex. "This is no time for personal vendettas."

"Dad, I have never asked for your help in anything like this before," Alex said.

"Do you think that killing these guys will bring Gabriella back to you, Alex?" asked Enzo. "We must take care of the business at hand, first. We will go back and revisit this matter at another time. I promise you."

Enzo walked to the other side of the room and took a cigar out of his humidor. He reached into his pocket looking for a lighter. Not finding one, he reached into his other pocket. "Anybody have a light?" he asked. Raul reached into his pocket and threw him a book of matches. "We have much work to do," he said.

Nunzio put his hands behind his head. "This could get bad," he said. "Raul, see what else you can find out on the street. Offer this girl some money if she can get you more information. We need names and things like that." He turned to his father. "Dad, I am going to that meeting with Tony's guys on Saturday. I'll travel to the meeting in a disguise. We need to know what Tony's next move is going to be. Ultimately, it affects us. I'll slip in the back way, nobody will see me."

"As much as I don't want you to go, I know it's the right thing to do," said Enzo.

Alex paced the room while the others spoke. His heart was filled with anger and his first reaction was to want to kill the ones who caused Gabriella's death. He realized, however, that as his father had said, there were other matters that would have to take precedent over his desire for vengeance. He was torn inside. His calling was to study medicine and save lives and yet he wanted to take another's life. He thought to himself that if Raul would supply him with the names of the two men involved in Gabriella's death he would kill them himself. Perhaps he could tell Tony and, surely, he would have them both murdered. He knew that any moves outside of the family could contain potential risk for himself and his family. He would wait. He would think later after his emotions had subsided and he was able to think logically and reason. Then he would see if he still felt the same.

The others in the room were talking, but Alex was not listening. His mind had drifted off to his own thoughts, dealing with his emotions and thinking about Gabriella. Minutes later, his mind drifted back to the room.

"Why can't we reverse the wire we found so we can listen in on these guys' conversation?" he asked Raul. "You got in there once, maybe you can get in again. Then we will know what the hell they are doing."

"Good idea, Alex," Nunzio said. "Who knows, we might learn something."

"Can we bug the house?" asked Alex.

"Al Ganado can help you with that," said Enzo. "He has friends in the business of security and surveillance. While you are at it, bug the tree at the sausage stand, too."

"What tree?" asked Nunzio.

Enzo replied. "The one the Hispanic guys sit under at the sausage stand." Everyone looked at him with a quizzical look. "There is a table that sits under a tree behind the sausage stand. Last time I went, I sat there myself. I was picturing in my mind these two shits sitting under the table discussing Tony. You know, like the sausage man, Luigi, said. I think to myself, I hope some bird shits in these bastard's sandwiches and they choke to death. If a bird can sit in the tree why can't a bug?" Enzo gestured with his hands. "Did you not notice the tree?"

Alex replied. "He's right, there is a tree there. That would be better than having to rely on Luigi to get us information."

"Good thinking," said Stefano. "So when we find out who is busting our balls do I get to kill these bastards?"

"First things first," replied Nunzio.

"You got work to do, what is everybody waiting for?" asked Enzo.

"You guys get going, me and Alex want to speak to the don alone," said Nunzio.

Raul and Stefano headed to the door; Stefano turned back and said, "I don't think anybody in the family called you that before. The don, Don Enzo, sounds pretty good." He headed back out and joined Raul upstairs.

"I assume you want to discuss your mother since you waited for the others to leave," said Enzo.

"No, it's not Mom we want to discuss, it's this thing of ours," said Nunzio.

"What thing?" asked Enzo.

"The business," replied Alex.

"The business," said Enzo, waiving his hands.

"Dad, me and Nunzio think it's time to quit, time to get out. These guys, this new breed coming up, they're ruthless. You can't deal with them. They don't care how many people they take out," said Alex. "It's happened in other cities. The black guys, the spics, the Russians. They are all getting into the business. They have the drug money; they will buy all your guys. They will control the streets. They pay better and they aren't afraid of the Feds. The guys that control the narcotics trade got the muscle."

"It's been a good ten years," replied Enzo. "You and Nunzio don't need this. I see things changing. I never thought things would get out of hand. After Tony and me worked things out I thought everything would always be quiet. I guess I was wrong."

"We all got complacent," said Alex.

"To quit now would create problems for us; it could be taken as a sign of weakness not only by these Loco Loco guys, but by Tony, as well," Enzo said. "Tony could turn on us if he thinks we sold out to these bastards. Let Nunzio go to the meeting, and then we can decide our next move. I did not want to say it in front of my brother Stefano, but if we have to retaliate we should not fool around with the little guys. We need to hit the big guys like this Soft Daddy guy. That will put their organization in disarray. If we need to do this, get Uncle Joe to handle it. Leave Stefano out of it."

"Won't you be digging a bigger hole for us?" asked Alex.

"If they won't talk to us we will have no choice. We have to hit them hard and at the top. It will shake out the little guys. Later we can discuss your proposal to disband this family. That is what you are asking me to do, isn't it?" asked Enzo. "I'm not so stupid to believe that this could have lasted forever. Besides who wants to deal with the Russians and all those other nationalities; they don't speak Italian. You are my sons and I love you, but we have to do this right. You can't just walk away."

"So you'll consider it?" asked Nunzio.

"When the time is right, when the time is right," said Enzo.

TWENTY-ONE

Tony had summoned the family leaders from several cities to attend the Saturday meeting. He had long-standing relationships with many of them through the circle of labor unions many of them headed. Representatives from cities like Rochester, Erie, Cleveland and Detroit had agreed to attend. Many of them had faced similar situations in their own cities and Tony hoped to gain some knowledge on how to approach his dilemma.

The meeting was to be held at Leo's Barbershop, a lower Westside establishment where many of the local wiseguys and union officials would get their hair cut. The barbershop had a back room, which was separated from the shop, itself, by a ceiling to floor curtain. Behind the curtain, on a back wall was a door. That door opened to a set of stairs, which led to a comfortable meeting room. The room contained a rectangular table, capable of seating ten people comfortably.

Nunzio had devised a plan to travel to the meeting incognito. There were some concerns in the Melina organization that the Feds might have the activities of the local mafia under surveillance. He would drive his car to a nearby mall and then take a taxi to the meeting site. He would pack a bag, containing a long coat and hat, which would easily hide his identity. He would slip the coat and hat on in the mall and then go back outside to catch a cab. After the meeting he would catch a ride back to the mall from one of the attendees, go back inside, ditch the coat and hat and proceed to his parked car.

Early that morning, Nunzio left his home and headed to the mall. He looked around to make certain that there were no suspicious vehicles in the neighborhood before driving away from his home. As he left his neighborhood, he made certain that he was not being followed. He arrived at the mall and executed his plan. He arrived at the barbershop, but before exiting the vehicle he asked the cab driver to please drive around the neighborhood a few times. He felt certain that the neighborhood was at least for now clear of any Feds. As planned, he entered the barbershop through a side door, wearing his coat and hat, which he then removed.

Leo, the barber, quickly greeted him. "Nunzio," he said, "good to see you again." He shook Nunzio's hand. "Go on down, you know where it's at. How about your Papa, is he coming?" he asked.

"No, just me today," Nunzio replied.

"You stop up here after the meeting, I'll get your haircut for you," replied Leo.

Nunzio replied. "If I have time, I'll do that, Leo." Nunzio proceeded through the curtain and down the stairs.

Tony warmly greeted Nunzio when he arrived in the meeting room.

"I'm so glad you could come, Nunzio. What about your father, will he be joining us today?" asked Tony.

"No, he will not. I will be representing the Melina family today," Nunzio said. "You know my old man, he hates meetings. He sends his greetings to all of his friends and associates."

Don Paolo Fabrizzu of Cleveland rose from his chair to greet Nunzio. "Do you remember me? You came to Cleveland with your father when you were about nine years old. I took you fishing on the lake."

"Don Fabrizzu, how could I ever forget the wonderful time I had? I think about it often," Nunzio said. "And how are you doing these days?" he asked.

Don Fabrizzu clasped his hands and said, "Like and old man who has seen better years. It's a bitch getting old. You'll see, you will get there, too." He then asked, "And your father, is his health good?"

Nunzio replied. "He is well, very well. I will tell him you asked about him."

"*Bene, bene,*" replied Don Fabrizzu.

Tony then grabbed Nunzio by the elbow and said. "Come here, I want you to meet Albert Lupo from Erie. I don't think you two have ever met."

"I don't believe we ever have," said Nunzio.

"Lupo, this is Nunzio, Enzo Mellina's son. Enzo runs some of my operations here," said Tony.

Nunzio was startled at the comment. He glanced over to Don Fabrizzu who seemed surprised at the wording of the statement, as well. Nunzio chose not to say anything at this time, not wanting to disrupt the meeting, which was about to begin.

"*Piacere,*" said Lupo as he hugged and kissed Nunzio.

"The pleasure is mine, sir," replied Nunzio.

All the participants sat down so the meeting could begin. Tony's *consiglieri*, Martin Eisman welcomed the participants. "Gentleman, thank you all for taking the time from your busy schedules to come here today. We hope that we can rely on you to advise us on how to handle the problem which has arisen here. From our previous conversations we understand many of you have faced this type of problem in your own territories. We hope to benefit from your past experiences. Tony would also like this to be a time to pledge to continue cooperation and respect for each other. It is a good time to renew our allegiances and undivided support of each other."

Eisman picked up a glass of water that was on the table in front of him and took a sip from it. He turned to Tony and said. "I will now turn the meeting over to the undisputed leader of our local chapter." Everyone then laughed. "Tony, it's all yours."

"Thank you all for being here today," Tony greeted the group. "As you know we have some new kids moving in on the block. We have learned that they are well-funded, ruthless and they like to kill people." Everyone laughed again. "It seems they are tied into a source from the Medeillin Drug Cartel. They are trying to muscle their way in on my business. Many of our past buyers are refusing to buy from us; these bastards are undercutting our price and threatening our customers. They kill cops and innocent children. Pretty soon the cops will be sniffing all of our asses. Gentleman, what do we do? We," he was interrupted by Tom Pignataro, boss of the Detroit mob.

"Tony, with all due respect. I was speaking with Martin earlier. It seems your plans are for us to wage an all out war against these sons-of-bitches in all of our cities. If that is what you are planning, I don't think that is in anyone's best interest. Yes, it would weaken their structure, but it would also get the Feds interested in our businesses again. I, for one, cannot afford that."

Tony replied. "Tom, you have not heard me out yet. Please let me finish! If we could band together and pull off a deal with the importers, we could limit the supply available to the distributors. That would choke them off. I don't believe they have allegiance to the distributors just because they speak Spanish. Money talks, they will sell to the highest bidder."

"What makes you think you can outbid them?" asked Don Fabrizzu. "From what my son has told me these people own the entire pipeline, from the field where it is grown to the distributor who sells it on the street. How can you compete with that?"

Albert Lupo now stated his view. "In my city we avoided getting into the drug trade. But as you know you cannot always control all the actions of your subordinates. Some of our guys, though loyal soldiers, found ways to make extra cash and lots of it by dabbling in narcotics. Tell you the truth, the *capos* didn't even know about it until two of our guys got whacked. Then we paid closer attention. We actually had one of our *capos* ask to leave the family so he could get into narcotics trafficking. He thought he was going to make millions. Two months later they found him dead. Dangerous business, this narcotics. At first, most people thought I had him clipped for leaving the family. Not so, we had an amicable parting and I am a man of honor. I honored our agreement. I did not interfere in his business as long as he stayed clear of our family. They never found who did it. Word on the street is that it was some young black kid. Lotsa balls these young kids. They don't give a shit who you are, they have no fear."

"I don't think hitting some of these punks in the street is going to clear the streets of your competition. They're like the fuckin' Energizer

Bunny; they keep going and going and going. Tony you know how much I love you but this is not like the old days. We no longer have the muscle or the money to finance a street war like that. The big families in New York and Jersey they still got it but it ain't like the old days. We have to pay so many people off these days it doesn't leave much to do anything else. Our families are smaller and so are our spheres of influence. For me, I'm content to keep what I have and avoid all the hassles. Let the spooks and spics do their drug thing. Their people go to jail every day in my city. They kill at least one of these guys every week. Most of it is black on black. Our people stay clean and out of jail. While my business is smaller, it's still there."

Tom Pignataro spoke again. "Tony, the best thing I can offer all of us is this advice. These problems are local. They need to be handled at a local level. Once we start crossing state lines the Feds are going to jump in. Then what?"

Don Fabrizzu stood up and said, "Is Tony going to get our people out of jail? Is he going to pay our legal fees?" Tony sat quietly. Don Fabrizzu continued. "What Tony is asking is socialism. Tony you have more to gain than most of us here if we support you in this."

Tony replied. "I also have the most to lose if something goes wrong. All these years we have known each other and some of you think that I would take advantage of you. What kind of bullshit is that?"

"No one is saying that you would take advantage here, Tony," said Don Fabrizzu.

"Then what the fuck are you saying?" shouted Tony.

"Take it easy, Tony," exclaimed Martin.

"Take it easy, my ass," said Tony. "Gentleman, I asked you here in the hopes that we might be able to join forces, to fight a common foe, keep the grounds fertile for us all." He shook his head and took a deep breath. "What I am hearing here is that Italians and Sicilians, people that share a common heritage, are not willing to help each other any longer."

Tom Pignataro responded. "It is not that we are not willing to help, it is that we can longer take the risks we used to take many years ago. Times have changed, Tony. You must understand that. Not all of us here trade in narcotics."

"Gentlemen, thank you for your time," Tony said. "I will go at this alone. I believe we have nothing more to talk about." He quickly exited the room, followed by his *consiglieri,* Martin Eisman. The others remained seated and somewhat stunned by Tony's actions.

Nunzio stood to bid the others goodbye. When he kissed and hugged Don Fabrizzu, the don whispered to him, "Wait outside, we need to speak." Nunzio went outside and waited for the don.

As Nunzio walked the don to his car, the don said to him, "You must come to my hotel so we can speak. It is too risky here. I think you will find what I have to say very interesting. Room 216, Statler Hilton. I'll wait for you there."

"I'll be there within the hour," replied Nunzio.

Nunzio called for a cab and headed back to the mall. He went inside to the restroom, ditched his coat and hat and went to his car. He immediately drove to the hotel to meet Don Fabrizzu. He entered the hotel and went to a house phone. After calling the don's room to announce his arrival, he headed to room 216. He knocked on the door and was greeted by the don's bodyguard. "Come in," he said, "the don is waiting for you."

"Nunzio come in and sit down," the don said.

Nunzio sat down as the don's bodyguard exited the room.

"Thanks again for coming," the don said as he sat next to Nunzio, squeezing his knee. "I heard about the attempted hit on your father the other night, thank God he was not hurt."

"He's fortunate," said Nunzio.

"Any ideas on who could have done it?" asked the don.

"We think this black drug dealer who calls himself Soft Daddy had something to do with it," replied Nunzio. "They think Dad and Tony are all one family and so they tried to hit Dad."

"So you think this devil is black," said Don Fabrizzu. "What else have you considered?"

Nunzio shrugged his shoulders. "That seems like the most logical conclusion."

The don again squeezed Nunzio's knee. "Tony has been playing both sides of the fence," he said to Nunzio. "He has been in Mexico and

Central America on so-called union business. What he has really been doing is trying to get the cartel guys to support him in a partnership with these black and Latin dealers. It seems that Tony is going to align himself with whoever gives him the better deal. After today, we know who that will be."

"I don't get it," said Nunzio.

"Tony has always gone for the home run. He wants to control the narcotics trade in this part of the country. He needs financing and someone to cover his back. His aspirations are almost as big as his ego," said the don.

"I felt Tony was disrespectful to my father when he said my father runs one of his operations. That's my dad's operation, not his," said Nunzio.

"Nunzio, the devil comes in many colors and sizes," said the don. "You should ask yourself, who has the most to gain by getting rid of your father." He stood up and placed his hand on Nunzio's shoulder. "Sometimes the enemy is closer to you than you think. Tony wanted our muscle to cut down the local guys so he could go to the cartel guys and say, okay your guys on the street are gone, now your only option is to deal through me. He becomes the big cheese then and before long takes over our families. Tony is power hungry and greedy. I don't put anything past him."

"You certainly have given us a lot to think about," said Nunzio. He stood and embraced Fabrizzu. "Thank you for your valuable insight."

"Tell my good friend, Enzo, to be careful," he responded.

Nunzio left the room and drove back home.

TWENTY- TWO

Nunzio made arrangements to meet with Enzo later the next day. The things that Don Fabrizzu told him earlier were weighing heavily on his mind. What bothered him even more was the comment that Tony had made to Albert Lupo in regards to his father. It was a well-known fact that Tony had a very big ego, until now Nunzio did not realize just how big it was. Was Tony so power hungry that he would try to take over the families of his lifelong friends and associates? Could Tony possibly be behind the attempt on Enzo's life? All of it just did not make sense. Tony would be taking a big risk turning his back on people he could trust to get in bed with people he had very few, if any, dealings with. Furthermore, he would be risking his own life if the others caught on to his scheme.

Nunzio had asked Raul earlier in the week to get his guys back into the house on Millner Avenue. He asked him to make copies of all the videos and voice recordings that had been shot of Tony's House. Perhaps there would be something on those tapes indicating what Tony was up to. He called Raul to ask if he had completed the task. Raul acknowledged that the copies had been made and he had them in his possession. He agreed to meet Nunzio at Enzo's on Sunday to deliver the tapes. Nunzio called Alex and Stefano to invite them, as well. It was agreed all would meet for a late lunch at Enzo's.

After speaking with Nunzio, Enzo called ahead to the Zarcone Meat Market to place an order for his made-to-order sausage. Fennel, cheese, and black pepper was the way Enzo liked his sausage made. Anthony Zarcone, one of the proprietors agreed to deliver Enzo's five-pound order later that day.

When Nunzio, Alex, Raul and Stefano arrived, Enzo was out in his yard grilling sausages. The aroma was noticeable blocks away and was enough to make anyone hungry. When the men walked into the house Enzo's bodyguard chuckled and said, "I hope you guys save me a piece of that sausage. It makes you salivate just smelling the stuff."

Alex turned to him and said, "We'll fix you up, don't worry."

Enzo had prepared quite a spread. On the table was *caponata* or eggplant appetizer, roasted red peppers, fresh baked sausage buns, fried potatoes with onion, corn on the cob and cannoli's for desert. The table would not have been complete without Enzo's homemade wine.

"*Minghia*, are you feeding an army?" asked Stefano, looking at the feast in front of him.

"I hope you guys are hungry," responded Enzo.

Nunzio started to say "I haven't seen a spread like this in this house since…" Suddenly, he stopped.

Enzo looked at him and said, "Since your mother left."

"Sorry, Dad," said Nunzio.

"Eat my sausage, it will make you forget about your mother," said Enzo.

"Wow, look at all this food," Alex said. "Let's eat."

"Sounds good to me," said Raul. The men sat at the table and helped themselves to the food. Enzo poured wine for all of them.

"So how was the meeting?" asked Enzo, looking at Nunzio.

"Short and not so sweet," replied Nunzio.

"How short?" asked Enzo.

"Like fifteen minutes short," replied Nunzio.

Alex said, "Doesn't sound like it went too good."

"I'm still a little puzzled by Tony's actions and his comments," Nunzio said. "He brings everybody together and when he doesn't get the answer he wants he dismisses everyone. Seems like his counselor, this Martin Eisman guy, was pleading Tony's case to these guys long before they got to Buffalo. Basically, what Tony was looking for was for all the local guys to rub out the distributors on the street so the cartel would have to sell through him."

"Then he controls the market and the prices. He pays what he wants when he buys and gets what he wants when he sells," Enzo said. "Isn't that how it goes?"

"None of the guys would support him on it, so he abruptly ended the meeting," said Nunzio. "But what is really interesting is what Fabrizzu told me afterwards."

"Fabrizzu, isn't that the old guy from Detroit?" asked Stefano.

"Cleveland, he's from Cleveland," responded Enzo.

"Fabrizzu told me that Tony has been in Mexico and Central America talking with the cartel people. He's trying to get them to support him in a partnership with the blacks and Hispanics," Nunzio said. "Looks like one way or another he's gonna find a way to corner the drug market."

"Son-of-a-bitch is playing both sides," said Stefano.

"Yes, and he will align himself with whoever it is that gives him the muscle and the financing to control the market," said Nunzio.

Enzo replied, "Either way, there will be a war. If the families support him he will eventually try to take over their families when his power base has grown enough. If the blacks and Latinos do it, he will eventually double cross them, too. This is the play Tony has been waiting to make for a long time."

"He realizes that's where the money is," said Alex.

"It's not the money he's after," said Enzo. "It's the power. He thinks he can be as big as John Gotti."

"There's more, Dad," said Nunzio. "Don Paolo eluded to the fact that perhaps it was Tony who called the hit on you." The room became strangely quiet.

"What…," said Stefano. "I think the old man is getting senile. As much as I don't like Tony, I don't think he has anything to gain by getting rid of my brother."

Raul who had been sitting quietly listening now offered his thoughts. "I think he is close to making the deal with the cartel guys. Now he no longer needs the boss's Canadian guys. He can buy the stuff cheaper, direct from the cartel, no middleman, and more money for him. So he either uses the other families to get rid of the black and Latino guys or he uses the black and Latino guys to help get rid of the family guys. When he's done there he gets rid of everybody else. This would not surprise me."

"Let's take the fucker out now," said Stefano. "This piece of shit is nothing but trouble for us. If we wait too long he will get the upper hand."

"Let's listen to the tapes before we decide anything," said Alex.

"Good idea, lets not jump the gun here," said Enzo.

"Let's finish eating, then we'll spend the rest of the day analyzing the tapes," said Nunzio. The men continued their meal and then split up to listen to the tapes. They played each voice recording of Tony's phone conversations and watched the videotapes that were covertly recorded. Several hours later they reassembled as a group to share their thoughts.

"So what have we got, guys?" Enzo asked.

"The usual stuff, like Tony's street guy reporting the day's take," said Nunzio, "Tony bitching about the street value of the drugs and wanting to rub out the new dealers. Nothing earth shattering or conclusive. Some babe always calling him, telling him what a good lover he is. That's about it."

"Alex, what about you?" asked Enzo.

"Tony's out to get these guys who used to work for him and are out doing their own thing now," said Alex. "He wants them all dead. He said he's going to wait for the right time, and then he's going to plug Soft Daddy. He said he's a pain in his ass that he needs to get rid of. The last tape I listened to was interesting. I can't put a time to it and I don't know who he is talking to, but he's giving an order to go through with the hit that he told them about earlier. I can't find anything in any of the other tapes referring to a hit. Anybody got any ideas?"

Nunzio replied, "Could be Soft Daddy, and could be Pops. Who knows?"

"Unless we are missing some of the tapes there doesn't seem to be very much there," said Alex. "Nothing very conclusive."

"Raul, what about you?" asked Enzo.

"I listened to the tapes we made on the guys on Millner," said Raul. "They got a bunch of amateurs working over there. You can tell listening to the conversations. They are going to deliver about 50 kilos a week here for processing. Anybody here read lips?"

"Why? You want to hire some deaf and dumb guys?" asked Stefano.

"I've got quite a good video of Tony talking; long conversation but no audio," said Raul. "The microphone must not have picked it up. Very clear video, just no sound."

"Let me take a crack at it," said Alex. Alex went to the next room to view the video. The others soon followed him. Raul played the video for Alex. Alex asked him to rewind and replay several times. A few minutes later Alex spoke.

"Wow! Big time shit," said Alex. "I don't know who he is talking to but he talked about offering these cartel guys arms for drugs. He said that was the one thing the black guys could not get their hands on. Does anybody recognize the other guy sitting by the pool?"

"Never seen him before," said Nunzio.

"No idea," said Stefano.

"He looks Hispanic. Let me show it to some of my guys, maybe somebody will recognize him," said Raul.

"Where is Tony going to get arms from?" asked Stefano.

"From the Russians," replied Alex.

"The Russians?" said Enzo.

"Their country is in such disarray that they can't control where their weapons are going. Since the Soviet Union broke up there have been a lot of stolen weapons on the market. You name it they got it. Shoulder fired missiles, RPGs, machine guns, everything," said Alex.

"What's an RPG?" asked Enzo.

"Rocket propelled grenade," said Nunzio.

"And what would they do with these arms?" asked Enzo.

"Use them in civil wars in Latin America and places like that. Give them to rebels so they can use them to destabilize the governments there. Someday they might get their hands on a nuclear device then we are all in trouble," said Alex.

"So that's Tony's edge," said Nunzio. "Now he's going to be a fuckin' arms dealer. I 'have read where there is a lot of this shit going on, this arms dealing stuff. Big bucks, too."

"This guy's a maniac," said Stefano. "Let's take him out now."

"What about the bug at the sausage stand, anything there, yet?" asked Enzo

"Not yet," said Raul.

As he was speaking Enzo's bodyguard interrupted the conversation. "Excuse me, boss, one of Raul's guys is here to see him. He said it's important."

"Send him in," said Enzo. A few seconds later one of Raul's accomplices entered the room.

"Bad news, boss," he said. "Me and Cruz were making the pickup from last week's bets. These guys come out of nowhere, come up behind us and shoot Cruz in the back of the head. He's dead boss. They took the box with the money, too. I saw him point the gun at me and I dove. The shot just missed me. Then they took off."

"Ever see these guys before?" asked Raul.

"Never," he replied.

"What about a car? Did you see a car?" asked Raul.

"White car, small. A Toyota, I think," he replied.

"That's what Luigi has said one of the Loco Loco guys who hangs out at the stand drives," said Alex.

"Raul, you think these guys could have been Hispanic?" asked Enzo.

"No doubt about it," said Raul.

"Okay, Stefano, here is your chance to get your hands dirty," said Enzo. "If these guys show up at Luigi's…" He pointed at Raul's guy. "He can identify them, let's take them out. Get those Colombian guys from Rochester to do it. They won't make a connection to us that way. Then we sit and wait until we get better information from all this other shit we got going on. Sooner or later we are going to get lucky and hear something good."

"I'm going to go down and see Luigi, see if there's anything new there," said Alex. "I'll see you guys later." Alex left Enzo's and drove directly to the sausage stand. He arrived to find a noticeably upset Luigi.

"Hey, Luigi, what's the matter?" asked Alex. "You look upset."

"They come here and eat, then they no pay for the food," said Luigi to Alex.

"Who?" asked Alex.

"The *Porto Rico* Mexican guys," said Luigi.

"They left without paying?" asked Alex.

"Bastards," replied Luigi. "They talk a lot when they was sit at the table. I give you the tape." Luigi went inside the sausage stand and retrieved the tape for Alex.

"Thanks, Luigi," said Alex as he accepted the tape from Luigi. As Alex turned to walk away, he noticed a man walking towards him. As the figure approached, Alex realized it was Joelle's father.

"Hey Tom, did you come to get a sausage from Luigi?" asked Alex.

"Love it, it's so good," replied Tom. "Alex, while you are here, if you have a minute, I would like speak with you."

Alex replied, "Get your sandwich, we can sit at a table and talk." Tom ordered his sandwich. When it was ready, he sat at a table with Alex to eat. After finishing his food he spoke to Alex.

"I'm glad I ran into you here. You probably think I want to talk to you about Joelle. That's not what I want to talk to you about," said Tom.

"So what's on your mind?" asked Alex.

"This is really not my business and I am not trying to be nosy and intrude. I know about the family thing, you know like what you read in the paper," said Tom. "For whatever it's worth I wanted to give you some heads up on something that I heard."

"Mostly what you read in the paper is crap," said Alex.

"Alex, I know you know my brother, Nick, and who he works for," said Tom. "There is something big going down here, it has something to do with conspiracy and corruption legislation."

"You mean RICO," said Alex.

"I guess that's it," said Tom. "Anyhow, some big guns from D.C. are coming in. I heard they are going to get all those guinea bastards off the street. I don't care what happened between you and Joelle, I still like you. You are the father of my grandchildren. I don't want to see you get hurt. Take it for whatever you feel it's worth." Tom picked up his trash and walked to the trash receptacle to deposit it.

Alex stood up and walked over to Tom. "Tom, thanks for caring," he said.

Tom nodded and walked away. He left Alex wondering about the discussion that Nunzio, Alex and Enzo had about winding down the family business. It was becoming apparent to Alex that based on what Tom had just said, the decision to get out may not be voluntary. The question remained, at what price?

TWENTY-THREE

Things were beginning to move quickly on the local scene. It seemed the threat to the Melina family was coming from three sides, Tony, the Loco's and now the Feds. It wasn't long before the duo that had hit Raul's collectors were themselves dead. The Colombians from Rochester had done their job avenging their death. Tony had put a hit out on some of the young black dealers who were working for Soft Daddy. The body count was suddenly rising. All of this activity was becoming noticed in the community. The newspapers were full of theories about what exactly was happening in the local underworld organizations. The organizations were right where they did not want to be... in the spotlight. It was apparent that a struggle for power had begun.

In the meantime, the FBI and U.S. Marshall's office intensified their efforts to break the back of the local families operations. One of Tony's button men was arrested on a conspiracy to commit murder charge. As word got back to Tony of the arrest, Tony was worried that the government would try to cut a deal with his button man in exchange for information on Tony. While his knowledge of Tony's operation was limited, he knew enough for the Feds to build a case under the RICO statutes. Tony had to act quickly before the prisoner could be transferred from local custody to federal custody. He could not afford to take any chances. He made arrangements for the prisoner to be killed before he could offer information to the authorities. The killing was arranged with the local prison guards who were on watch at the jail. It was made to look like a botched escape attempt so that no one would question the death.

The search for answers as to who called for the hit on Enzo now intensified. Every source available to the Melinas was being utilized to find out who had called the hit. The house on Millner Avenue was placed on twenty-four hour surveillance and any pertinent information from the surveillance or the bugged telephone line was immediately reported back to Nunzio. Any tidbit of information anyone obtained from any source, no matter how trivial it seemed was given to Nunzio.

Alex had conveyed to the others what his father in law had told him about the FBI and US Marshall's activities. There was a nervous air about the entire family. Things seemed so uncertain now. The heat and pressure was definitely on. The worry was apparent in everyone's faces.

The surveillance team on Millner Avenue reported back that the empty propane tank that had been delivered to the house on Millner had been recently filled with propane. Deliveries to the house began to increase. Raul was certain that the unrefined narcotics had begun to pour in for processing. The operation was now in full swing.

It appeared that the two men who were responsible for Gabriella's death spent most of the time at the Millner Avenue address. Their job apparently being to keep the house secure. The house was now occupied around the clock. It was impossible to get back into the house as it was constantly occupied.

It was decided that in light of what was learned about Tony, it would not be a good idea to attempt to make contact with Soft Daddy. Nunzio had wanted to explain that Enzo and Tony ran separate operations and that Enzo was of no threat to the Loco's or Soft Daddy. If any information leaked out to Tony about any meeting between the Melinas and the Loco's or Soft Daddy, he would suspect that Enzo was aligning himself against Tony. It was too much a risk to take.

So the killings continued. Six people in all were killed over the next three months. This was more than had been killed in the last ten years combined. With the Feds closely monitoring the activities of the mob in Buffalo, most illegal activities slowed down significantly. This slow down created a large dent in the mobs cash flow and was putting a strain on the organizations from top to bottom. The judges, politicians, and police captains on Enzo's payroll still expected their monthly payments. Those within Enzo's organization had to be paid as well. Enzo could not afford to lose the people who had helped him build his organization. He decided to use revenues from his development company to temporarily fund his other activities. This was a risky move because transactions from his corporate bank accounts could come under the scrutiny of the IRS. There was no doubt that this was the most difficult crisis the Melina organization had ever dealt with.

While the situation seemed bleak, there would be some good news. The surveillance and eavesdropping on the Loco's would finally pay off. Luigi the sausage man had called Nunzio to report that a long meeting involving several people had taken place behind his sausage stand. He suggested to Nuzio that he come quickly to pick up the recording. Nunzio raced to the stand to pick up the tape. While nothing significant was heard on the last tape that Alex had picked up, this one would prove to be an eye opener. Although primitive in nature, the recording device was doing its job and was beginning to pay dividends.

The contents of the recording revealed that Soft Daddy was planning to take out both Enzo and Tony. The Loco's were well aware of Tony's moves in Mexico and Central America. Soft Daddy felt it was time to move against Tony, before he could solidify his relationship with the cartel members. While Soft Daddy had learned that Enzo was not involved in Tony's narcotics dealings, he felt that because of Enzo's power base and his relationship with mafia leaders in other cities, he could pose a threat to him in the future. He simply could not afford to have him around, so he ordered his killing as well.

Meanwhile the question of who had made the initial attempt on Enzo's life was also answered. Nunzio learned that Tony had used hired guns to try to assassinate Enzo. Because the hit on Enzo was not successful, Tony refused to pay the assassins the remaining half of the hit fee. This angered the hired assassins who refused to carry out the assassinations of the family leaders in other cities. They intentionally leaked the information to people close to the Melina family. What was ironic was that Soft Daddy had hired the same hit men to assassinate Tony and Enzo that Tony had used to try and eliminate Enzo.

It became clear that Tony's master plan was to eliminate the family leaders in the surrounding cities and overrun their operations. He could then use his cartel connections to control the narcotics trade in a vastly large region of the country. His lust for power would be fulfilled. He would have no opposition to his dealings. He would turn his back on old friends and allies to accomplish his goals.

The Melina's had to act and act quickly. Nunzio sent word to the leaders in the other cities that their operations as well as their lives were in danger because of Tony's plans. The local police officials on the Melina family payroll were advised of the impending turf war between Tony and the Loco's. This would provide a cover for Enzo's plans to strike back at Tony as well as the Loco's.

Enzo was taken to a remote hunting lodge in Canada where he would remain under the protection of his old friend Dominick until it would be safe for him to return to Buffalo. Nunzio would run the everyday operations in his absence, sending him periodic updates.

Tony was well aware of the increased scrutiny by the FBI as well. This did not seem to bother him and while his counter parts were lying low, Tony seemed to intensify his activity. He pressed on to eliminate those he felt stood in his way of absolute control of the narcotics trade.

Don Fabrizzu, Enzo's old friend had called Nunzio later that month to deliver some important news.

"Nunzio I got word your father is away on an expedition," said Don Fabrizzu.

"He wanted you to know he is all right," replied Nunzio.

"I understand the heat is still on up there," said Fabrizzu.

"We're trying to stay under the radar here," answered Nunzio. "It's really put a dent in the cash flow. Everybody here is pretty nervous. We're trying to hold it together until we can find a way out. We can't just walk away yet."

"I think the curtain is coming down quickly for all of us," replied Fabrizzu. "It has been a good run. It's no longer like in the old days. These non-*paesans*, they would betray their own mothers. You can't trust anyone these days." He took a deep breath. "I have some interesting news for you. Some of our friends in the trucking industry made some big dollars picking up crate loads of arms at one of the ports in Jersey. Word is the shipment is headed to Buffalo."

"That's interesting," replied Nunzio. "I bet I know the fuckin' army general who ordered it too."

"I think your general is headed towards his Waterloo," said Fabrizzu.

"My guess is he'll trade for narcotics," said Nunzio.

"Good guess," said Fabrizzu.

"Obviously you know more," said Nunzio.

Fabrizzu continued. "This stupid bastard has double crossed so many people it wont be long before he has more enemies than friends. His problem is he doesn't know it yet. He has a truckload of stuff coming from Mexico. Coca Cola. We got a mole to infiltrate his family. We're getting some good information from him."

"You got good sources, Don Fabrizzu," replied Nunzio.

The don laughed and said, "I'm old, I can still see and hear. I've made a lifetime staying close to my friends and staying even closer to my enemies. Nunzio, Tony is going to move against us all in the next thirty days. He is bringing in guys from the cartel to help him. Time is running short. Every family needs a plan to deal with this. I hope you guys are ready. Tell my friend Enzo his old friend is fine and the old warrior isn't going down without a fight. When all this bullshit is behind us, I want you and your father to come up here. We'll go for a ride on my boat. Bring the doctor too."

"This bastard is going down, the question is who gets to him first," said Nunzio. "We're ready, just waiting for the right moment." The conversation continued for several more minutes as Don Fabrizzu supplied Nunzio with more information on what he had learned about Tony's activities.

"We'll talk on the other side of hell," said the don to Nunzio as he hung up the telephone.

Nunzio quickly summoned Alex and Raul to his home to discuss the information he had obtained from Don Fabrizzu. In his own mind, he was already formulating a plan on what the family's next move should be. With Enzo in hiding and in virtual isolation, the burden of making the decisions would rest squarely on Nunzio's shoulders. He realized there was no time to wait; it was time to act and act decisively.

Alex and Raul arrived a few hours later at Nunzio's house. Rosie greeted them at the door and sent them to the kitchen where Nunzio was waiting for them.

"You guys want something to eat or drink?" asked Nunzio.

"Pepsi," replied Raul.

"Water," said Alex.

"You guys hungry? We got all kinds of stuff here to munch on," said Nunzio.

"We're okay," said Alex.

Nunzio started into the conversation. "I had a long talk with Fabrizzu today. His people got some pretty good information on Tony and his activities." Nunzio sipped from the glass of water before him on the table. "Looks like Tony has a truck load of illegal arms on the way here from Jersey. He also has some coke coming in through Mexico."

"Drugs for arms, this guys got balls," said Alex.

"It gets better," said Nunzio. "Looks like he's going to make his move against everybody in the next thirty days."

"Who's everybody boss?" asked Raul.

Nunzio replied. "Us, Fabrizzu, Lupo, Pignataro, the big spook. He has got a bullet for all of us."

"I still don't see why he needs guys like Pignataro, Lupo and Fabrizzu out of the picture," said Alex.

"He wants to control all those organizations, he doesn't want to co-exist with them," replied Nunzio.

"Not the kind of guy who wants to look over his shoulder all the time," said Alex.

There was a silence for several seconds. Nunzio began to speak again.

"Tony got some guys from the cartel to come in to carry out the hits. Our job is to disrupt his plans. We need to come up with something and fast."

"I hear from my Latino brothers that there is a meeting at the factory on Millner on Saturday morning," said Raul. "All the Loco guys and some of Soft Daddy's people going to be there."

"You remember the girl Natale tore up, you know the one we helped out, the one in the videos?" asked Alex.

Nunzio gesturing with his hands asked, "What's she got to do with it?"

"Every once in a while she calls to give us some tidbits of information. She heard that the Loco guys are meeting with some guys from Colombia at this meeting on Millner," said Alex. "That's interesting because the cartel guys are aligned with Tony. My guess is these guys from Colombia she is referring to is the hit squad Tony is bringing in. My guess is that Tony had the cartel set up a meeting with the Loco's under false pretenses so he could plug them all at the meeting."

"Slick bastard," said Nunzio. "I think your guess is right on Alex. How convenient, have all the top guys in one place at one time. Shit!"

"Maybe that's a good thing for us too boss," said Raul. "Tony and Soft Daddy both want to get Enzo right? So we draw first blood."

"That will really cause some confusion wont it?" said Alex.

"So how do you propose we do this Raul?" asked Nunzio.

Raul replied, "I told you we can't get inside because they always have those two guys in the house right. But outside is a different story. There is no perimeter lights or alarms on the property. So we can do something at night, when it's dark."

"Like what?" asked Nunzio.

"When they put in the propane tank, they cut a hole in the cinder block so they can run the refill pipe down to the tank," Raul said. "They cut the hole real big and used a small pipe. There is a good size hole leading down to the tank. We can slide some C-4 down the pipe close to the tank, then adios!"

"Let's light these mother's asses on fire," said Alex.

"Set it up," said Nunzio. Nunzio turned to Alex. "I think it's time to make a deal with the FBI."

"What kind of deal?" asked Alex.

"You know when all this shit goes down they're going to be looking for dad. He's going to get nailed with the rest of them," said Nunzio. "If we can find out where the weapons are going to be delivered, you can try to cut a deal with your wife's uncle. The FBI gets the weapons and Tony, the old man walks free."

"How do you know he has the authority to do that?" asked Alex.

"If he doesn't he'll find who does," replied Nunzio. "We can't hide the old man in the woods forever.

"That only leaves Soft Daddy," said Raul.

Nunzio replied, "If Tony doesn't get him first, we'll have to do it ourselves.

"So is that when we all get out Nunz?" asked Alex.

"Hey, you're pretty smart for a doctor brother," said Nunzio.

Alex put his arm around Raul. "Make sure those two fuckers who caused Gabriella's death are in the house when you light it."

TWENTY-FOUR

Saturday was fast approaching and Raul had managed to get the explosive charge on the pipe leading to the propane tank. Nunzio received word from Fabrizzu's mole as to where the illegal arms would be stored before the exchange was made. Tony's people had chosen an old warehouse on Plymouth Avenue to store the crates of weapons until the coke shipments arrived from Mexico. At that time, the drugs would be exchanged for the illegal arms. Tony would pay the two million dollar difference in cash to the coke supplier.

The old warehouse was the perfect place for storing the illegal weapons. The three-story building was an old freight storage terminal, which could accommodate semi trailer trucks on the ground level. It had large concrete driving ramps to give smaller trucks and fork lifts access to the second and third floor storage levels. The trucks delivering the arms as well as the drugs could drive into the building where the exchanges would be made in an enclosed area out of the public eye. There would be little or no reason for anyone in the neighborhood to have any suspicion as to what was going on inside.

Alex contacted his father in law and asked him to arrange a meeting with his brother Nick. He asked him to keep the request confidential and wanted it to be a one on one meeting between Alex and Nick. Within a few days Alex would have his meeting with Nick.

Alex had asked that Nick meet him at the hospital after his shift. When Nick arrived Alex invited him into the residents dorms. There they were met by Raul who politely asked Nick if he could search him for weapons or a wire. At first Nick objected but later went along with the request. Alex then asked Nick to walk outside on the hospital grounds where they could talk privately.

The two men began to stroll the hospital grounds. Nick began the conversation. "It's rather odd that the criminals are frisking the cops isn't it?" he asked Alex.

"Nick, I didn't ask you here to get into a pissing contest with you or try to undermine you or anything else," Alex said to him. "I think we can help each other here."

"What's on your mind doctor?" Nick asked.

"There is a lot of shit going on and even more coming down," Alex said. Most of it involves narcotics. I want to make something perfectly clear to you Nick. The Melina family is in no way shape or form not now, not before, nor ever will be involved in narcotics trafficking." Nick stopped walking for a moment.

"You ask for a meeting to tell me this. Why didn't you just put it in a letter or a Christmas card?" asked Nick.

"That's not why I asked for the meeting," said Alex. "I was hoping we could work something out. Make a deal of some sort."

"Ok, so what have you got and what do you want?" asked Nick.

"Nick some guys tried to whack my old man not too long ago." Alex said. "I'm sure you fed guys know all about it already. There's a lot of shit you guys don't know. That's where I can help you."

"For a price, right?" Asked Nick.

Alex nodded in the affirmative. "Yeah for a price, nothing is free anymore."

"Go on, talk to me doctor," said Nick.

"There are going to be attempts on other people lives in other cities. There is a big turf war for narcotics happening now and it's going to get bigger," said Alex. "It involves a lot of people and it's not going to be pretty."

"They never are," said Nick smiling.

Alex continued. "Right here in our city there is a struggle taking place for control of the narcotics distribution market. You have two groups that are going to try to wipe the other ones out."

"Good for them, then we won't have to feed and clothe the bastards in prison with our tax dollars," said Nick. Nick became angry. "Stop bullshitting, cut to the chase Alex. What the hell do you want and what do you have to give for it? It's that easy."

"I want protection for my father," replied Alex.

"Protection, like what, like body guards. I thought you guys had your own bodyguards," said Nick.

"Immunity Nick, I want immunity for him," said Alex.

Nick stopped again. "I guess I'm a little confused. You just told me your old man is not involved in the narcotics trade and now you want immunity. If his hands are clean what are you worried about?"

"When all this shit hits the fan, the Feds will pull everybody off the street, no matter what they are involved in," Alex said. "I don't want my father lumped in with those guys, it's different."

"Why is it different? Crime is crime," responded Nick.

"Nick, the old thing, the Cosa Nostra it's over. We all realize that. My family has good legitimate business. They need some breathing room to make the transition," said Alex.

"So what's the deal you want to make?" asked Nick. "What do you have to offer?"

"My old man is in a protected place because of all this crap. When he comes back he's left alone. Overlooked, exonerated, whatever you care to call it," said Alex.

"Large demands," said Nick. "What's the carrot?"

"Information, information you don't have. Information could make you a hero. Maybe get you promoted or something like that," said Alex.

Nick's faced turned red with anger. "Don't patronize me you little shit. Get to the point here or this conversation is over."

"I can get you the names of everybody involved in the narcotics trade here and in other cities as well. I can get you information on sources, refining factories and who is getting ready to clip who," Alex said. "You might have some names, but what I can give you will help you put a much larger dent in these operations than you could do on your own. You could do it in half the time too." Alex looked at Nick and grinned. "If that doesn't interest you this will. Some of these narcotics are going to be traded for illegal weapons. I'm not talking small arms here. I'm talking RPG's and heavy stuff like that. You know the kind of shit they use in civil wars and terrorist activities."

Nick listened very attentively now. "Really," he said.

"The FBI does get involved in this kind of activity. Doesn't it Nick?" asked Alex.

"How do I know you're not bullshitting me?" asked Nick.

"Let's do this Nick. Let's talk again on Sunday," said Alex.

"Sunday, why Sunday?" asked Nick.

"Let's just say Saturday will be such a blast it will lend credence to the fact I know a little more than the Feds when it comes to some matters," replied Alex.

"Okay. Sunday will be good. It gives me a few days to think about your offer," said Nick.

"I'll meet you here at three o'clock on Sunday," said Alex.

"Agreed," said Nick as he shook Alex's hand. As he walked away he wondered what his next step should be. Should he go to his superiors at the FBI now or wait until Sunday's meeting to decide.

In the back of his mind he realized that what Alex had said to him about his getting recognition or promoted was in many ways accurate. Nick had been with the FBI for over twenty years but had never risen above the level of special field agent. If what Alex told him was true, this could be a big bonanza for him. He would have a hand in dealing a major blow to organized crime in the region. He would also have a hand in crippling the narcotics trade in a multi state area as well as stemming the flow of illegal arms to rebel groups or terrorists. He understood that a breakthrough of this magnitude would get him national attention as well.

Alex called Nunzio to inform him of the conversation he had with Nick. Nunzio was pleased with the fact that there was potential for them to cut a deal for Enzo. The stage was being set for the Melinas to make a clean break from the world of organized crime. The time to get out was now and with Nick's cooperation it would be an easy way out.

It would be extremely important that no one outside of the Melina family ever know that there was any cooperation between the Melinas and the FBI. The other families in this part of the country would not look upon this favorably. If not done secretly, it could create problems with the other families. It could arouse suspicion that the Melinas had passed information on to the FBI concerning the others families activities. Nunzio had no intention of giving the FBI any information other than what was needed to put Tony and Soft Daddy away. Both Alex and Nunzio slept well that night knowing that the end that they had hoped for was now within their reach. There still however remained some unfinished business to attend to.

Saturday arrived and Nunzio had set up a surveillance van just down the street from the house on Millner Avenue. The van was manned by two of Nunzio's best soldiers. The plan was to try and have as many of the principal players from the Loco's and Soft Daddy's crew comfortably inside before the explosive device on the propane tank was triggered remotely. The meeting was scheduled to begin at 11 a.m. First to arrive were three of Soft Daddy's top accomplices. Soon after, the top two people in the Loco organization arrived. Instead of going inside, they waited on the porch for others to arrive. They were soon followed by some of their street enforcers and other lowlifes. Last to arrive were Tony's hit men from the cartel. The stage was now set to blow the local drug trade into a state of mass confusion.

The occupants of the surveillance van would have to leave the area before the explosion could be triggered. The blast was expected to be powerful enough to blow apart the narcotics factory. It could conceivably cause some damage to the surrounding houses as well and it was certain there would be debris sent airborne over several acres of land. It would be too dangerous for the van to remain nearby to witness the blast.

The surveillance team waited patiently for two remaining participants who had not arrived. They were the two gang members who were involved in Gabriella's drowning and Alex was counting on their being present to receive their just reward. More than one hour had passed and still no sign of the two missing gang members. If the

Melinas waited too long to trigger the explosion, the cartel assassins could begin their hit and spoil the Melinas plans. They had waited long enough. It was time to leave the scene so the explosive device could be triggered. The van headed to the end of the cul-de- sac to turn around and head out of the neighborhood. On their way out of the neighborhood they noticed another vehicle entering the neighborhood. As they checked their rear view mirror looking back towards the neighborhood, they saw the car parking in front of the house on Millner Avenue. Minutes after leaving the neighborhood and now several blocks away they heard the blast from the propane tank. Their mission had been accomplished.

The explosion had been so strong that it blew the windows out of houses in a multi block area. The blast itself was heard several miles away. The house was completely leveled by the explosion and debris was sent flying over several blocks. When firefighters and emergency personnel arrived at the scene they were awed by the destruction they were witnessing. The house had been completely destroyed and was a burning ball of fire.

Firefighters worked quickly to put out the fire. After about one hour, the fire was contained. As investigators sifted through the smoldering rubble, they began to locate the bodies of the men who had occupied the house at the time of the explosion. They then discovered some gruesome finds. Body parts were strewn throughout the rubble. The force of the explosion had been so great that there were also body parts lying in the front yard of a neighboring house.

There was also one casualty from the neighborhood itself; a slightly retarded man known as Crazy Eddie. Crazy Eddie would drive his riding lawnmower through the neighborhood singing songs and yelling obscenities at the neighbors. The neighbors had learned to ignore him taking into consideration his mental state. He was simply at the wrong place at the wrong time and was hit by flying debris. He was killed instantly.

As the emergency personnel continued to sift through the pile of rubble, they found a man badly burned and clinging to life. He was immediately transported to a local hospital; it was the hospital where

Alex was on duty. As he was wheeled into the emergency room Alex who was on ER duty recognized who the man was. It was one of the men who were responsible for Gabriella's death. Alex's first inclination was to just walk away and not assist in helping to save the man's life. He struggled with his emotions but finally gave in and assisted the lead ER physician treating the badly injured man. After administering emergency medical treatment for over an hour the badly injured man succumbed to his injuries.

Alex felt a wide swing of emotions. As a physician he felt a sense of failure in not being able to save the man's life. Knowing that the man was responsible for Gabriella's death, he felt that justice had been served. He was visually shaken by the ordeal. The lead ER physician noticing the strain on Alex's face told him to take a break so he could collect himself. Alex took a thirty-minute break and returned to complete his shift.

After his shift, he went directly to Nunzio's house to watch the evening news and discuss the day's events. The local television stations were full of reports on the explosion. The body count was now in. Ten dead at the scene and one nearby fatality. Widespread damage was also reported to neighboring houses as well as broken windows over a multi block radius. Fortunately the explosion injured no one else in the neighborhood. One of the television stations was reporting that narcotic refining equipment was found in the rubble. The report went on to say that federal authorities were being called in to assist in the investigation.

Alex turned to Nunzio and said, "Damn, you guys sure did light up the sky. How much C-4 did you guys use?"

"I think it was all the flammable shit they had inside the place," Nunzio said. "Who the hell knew? I hope you can cut a deal with the FBI guy tomorrow so all this crap can come to an end." Nunzio sighed as he lit a cigarette. "Who ever knew that it would all come to this?" The room was silent for about a minute. Nunzio spoke again. "Then for this retarded guy to get hit by the door. How unlucky can you be?"

"Is that the guy on the lawnmower I heard about? He was retarded? Alex asked.

"Yeah, mentally challenged you could say," Nunzio said.

"Nunzio, what if the FBI won't cut a deal for the old man, then what?" Asked Alex.

Nunzio raised his eyebrows and responded. "Then Dominick helps us get him out of Canada and to Sicily. We can't hide him in the north woods forever. It's too dangerous for him to stay there."

Alex stood up to leave. "I'll call you tomorrow after the meeting," he said to Nunzio.

Nunzio walked him to the door. As Alex approached his car Nunzio yelled out to him. "Hey brother, keep your head up. It's almost over."

Alex shook his head and smiled. He got into his car and drove away.

TWENTY-FIVE

The next day Alex arose earlier than his usual time and went through his normal morning routine of showering, dressing and having his coffee. After about thirty minutes he was ready to head out the door when his telephone rang. It was Catalina calling. She asked Alex to meet her for breakfast. Since Alex was ready for work earlier than his usual time he agreed to meet her. It was obvious by the sound of her voice that there was something she needed to discuss with Alex. They agreed to meet at a local Denny's restaurant.

Alex was already seated and waiting by the time Catalina arrived. Alex stood up, hugged and kissed his sister on the cheek. He held her for a few seconds whispering in her ear. "It seems like ages since I've seen you sis, I miss you." Catalina smiled and pushed back the hair on Alex's forehead.

"I miss you too brother. You are always so busy with work and the boys."

"Where have all the years gone?" Alex asked.

"I don't know brother," replied Catalina. "Look at you now, a doctor. I'm so proud of you. So is mom and dad, we are all so proud of you."

"I could not have done this without my family's help and support," said Alex.

Catalina smiled. "I'm starving, let's eat," she replied.

The waitress approached as they sat down at the table. "What can I get you two this morning?" she asked. Catalina and Alex gave the waitress their orders and settled back into their seats.

"What's on your mind sis?" asked Alex.

"Trouble brother, trouble," she replied. Alex sat with a quizzical look on his face.

"Do you remember my friend Ruth at the DA's office?"

"Yeah," replied Alex. "I remember Ruth."

"I've got some pretty big information concerning Dad," Catalina said. "They're getting ready to indict him on multiple charges. The FBI has been in town with some Feds from the justice department. They are going to arrest him as soon as he comes back."

"Your friend tell you this?" he asked.

Catalina nodded yes as she fought back the tears. "Alex they know he's in Canada. Sooner or later they are going to find him and arrest him."

"What are the charges? Did she tell you what the charges are?" asked Alex.

"She didn't say," replied Catalina.

"Shit," said Alex pounding the table. "The bastard set me up."

"Who set you up? How?" asked Catalina looking directly at Alex.

"Look, I can't tell you much right now, not in here," whispered Alex. "I'm going to need your help with something soon. Can I count on you?"

"Anything for you and dad," she replied. A few moments later their breakfast orders arrived. They sat quietly through breakfast eating their food. Alex maintained a worried look on his face as he consumed his food. He wiped his mouth and leaned foreword to talk quietly to Catalina.

"I've got to get to my shift at the hospital and I have a meeting to attend after work," he said to her. "Get over to Nunzio's. Don't call him on the phone. Tell him to get dad out of the country now, not to wait."

Catalina replied. "But Alex, dad is out of the country. He's in Canada, remember?"

"Just tell him that," said Alex. "He will know what to do." Alex sighed as he grasped his sister's hand. "Tell him I'll be in touch with him soon."

"Alex, when is someone going to tell me what the hell is going on?" she asked her brother.

"Sis, I'm going to need you in a big way," Alex said. "I'll tell you everything real soon. I promise. No more secrets. It's time you knew the truth anyhow, okay."

Catalina hugged Alex. "I trust you Alex, I want you to know that."

"Love you, Cat," Alex said to her rising from the table and throwing down a few dollars for the tip. "Can you get the check?" he asked.

Catalina laughed. "Sure, I'll buy for my big shot doctor brother. Go on get to work, you're going to be late, go!" Alex blew her a kiss as he headed towards the door.

Alex arrived at the hospital twenty minutes later and began his shift. He had a difficult time staying focused on his work after getting the disturbing news from Catalina. He knew that Nick was going to double cross him in order to get to Enzo. Alex decided to play along and hear Nick out later that day. He would not let on that he knew anything about the forthcoming indictments. The hours seemed to pass so slowly. It was if as the hands on the clock were standing still, never moving.

Midway through his shift, an ambulance arrived at the emergency center. Alex was asked to assist in treating a young boy who had been hit by a car. His injuries were serious and there was no time to lose. The ER doctors sprang into action working feverishly to save the boys life. After about sixty minutes they had stabilized him enough to get him to surgery. There the surgical team would take over to complete the life saving process. Alex and the lead ER physician both headed to the scrub area to wash their hands and change their bloodied clothing.

"Good work today, Doctor Melina," the physician said to Alex. "You helped to save a young boy's life. You did very well under pressure. It's not easy when it's some little munchkin involved."

"No, not at all," replied Alex.

"Got kids?" asked the physician.

"Two, Two boys," replied Alex.

"Well go home and hug your kids tonight and tell them how much you love them," said the doctor. "Tell them what a good doctor their daddy is and how he saved some little guys life today. Your wife and kids can be proud of you doctor. You are good at what you do."

"Thanks," replied Alex. "That means a lot to me. You just gave me a good perspective to my life. Thanks."

The remainder of the shift now did not seem so long. Alex felt vindicated about his previous feelings when he was torn about helping one of Gabriella's killers in the ER. It was time to move on and make everything else about his life and his family right. In his mind, Alex was formulating a plan.

The end of his shift arrived and Alex headed out to meet with Nick. After exchanging greetings, Alex and Nick walked over to Luigi's Sausage Stand to sit down and talk.

"So do we have a deal?" asked Alex.

"That was some fireworks display last night, wasn't it doctor?" asked Nick. Alex shrugged his shoulders. "Your people have anything to do with that?" he asked.

"No, and I can prove it," replied Alex. "Do we have a deal?" he asked again.

"Talk to me doctor and your old man gets off free," said Nick.

Alex took a deep breath. "This is a little complicated so I'm going to give you some background information first. Tony Riccio has been in control of the narcotics trade here for several years, virtually unchallenged. Not too long ago the blacks and Hispanics who used to push the stuff on the street decided they wanted a bigger piece of the pie. This is something Tony was not willing to give up. Well those guys decided to find their own sources for the drugs and as you can imagine some friction developed. Pretty soon people started getting clipped over all this narcotics shit."

"And I guess you are going to tell me none of your people are involved in this," said Nick.

Alex let out a long sigh. "Let me finish Nick, let me finish. The Hispanic crew is a gang called the Locos. Most are players from Central America. They have aligned themselves with a black gang headed by some big black guy called Soft Daddy."

"I know Soft Daddy. He's got some pull in the music industry. He helps new artist's get audiences with some rap record labels," said Nick. "He's got a clean sheet."

"He's not as clean as you think he is Nick," said Alex. "He's involved in prostitution and the narcotics trade. He keeps himself well insulated from the action. Judging from how little your people know, I say he has done a pretty good job of it. Did you know he runs a few speakeasies here in town?"

Nick replied. "No, I did not know that, forgive my ignorance."

"Anyhow, Soft Daddy and the Locos are going to clip Tony if Tony doesn't get to them first," Alex said to Nick. "Are you starting to get this picture now?" he asked.

"Go on," Nick said. "This is getting interesting."

"Tony wants to be the big cheese so he doesn't want an influential person like my father around. Soft Daddy and the Locos think my old man and Tony are tied in together so they are trying to get to him too," Alex said.

"So that explains the attempted hit on your old man," Nick said.

"You got it," said Alex. "So that's why we are here today. My dad is not now nor was he ever involved in this narcotics thing. Nick, we are all well aware that this thing that the old country guys had is virtually dead. They don't control the real money industries like narcotics so they have lost virtually all their power. There has been a changing of the guard. They all know it. They are trying to slide out of the limelight gracefully. They certainly should not be of any concern to the Feds anymore. You guys got bigger fish out there to catch."

Nick shook his head and laughed. "So you think the government should be like the Catholic Church and have degrees of sin like venial and mortal. You think guys like your old man should have their sins classified differently than the Hispanics and blacks. Maybe say a few Hail Marys and a few Our Fathers and their sins forgiven. Is that how you immoral *goombas* look at it?"

Alex became disturbed at Nick's comments. "Is that any more immoral than getting caught by a co-worker with your penis in the office manager's mouth after business hours?" Nick was shocked at Alex's comments. Both men stared at each other for several seconds. Alex still angry continued to breath heavily.

"That was a mistake, an error in judgment," Nick replied.

"Yeah, but it was still adultery, immoral and, may I say, illegal," Alex said to Nick.

"So what are you, the fucking Pope now?" Nick yelled to Alex.

"And who are you, the fucking President?" Alex yelled back. Once again the men became silent and stared at each other. After a few moments Nick began to speak.

"I guess my niece told you all about my affair with the girl in the office."

"Let's just say there are not many secrets in your family, Nick," Alex said. "Anyhow that's not what matters here, that's not why we came here today."

"So what about the arms for drugs deal?" asked Nick.

"You need to have your people ready to move in quickly. I can't give you much notice. I can only tell you the exchange is going to be made in the suburbs, not in the city." Alex was clearly trying to throw Nick off of any location ideas he may have had.

"In the next seven days, you can get Tony and some of the cartel guys all at once. This is going to be some big stuff for your office Nick. Put you guys on the map. You'll not only put a dent in the regional drug trade you will also have a hand in slowing down terrorism and political instability in neighboring countries."

"All right. Your old man needs to come down and meet with us in our office," Nick said to Alex. "We will take him somewhere safe for a couple of weeks until all this blows over. I need him to come in first before we can do anything to help him."

Alex pointedly asked the question. "Are there any indictments pending against him now?"

Nick replied. "No, no, no. I tell you, I took care of all that. There won't be any problems at all." Alex realized Nick was lying to him, but played along. "A couple of weeks in a hotel and we will work everything out and get it all cleaned up. You have my word, Alex." Nick extended his hand to Alex and both men shook hands to close the deal.

Alex stood up to walk away. He said to Nick, "Send someone over to Riccio's pool house. You are going to find some wires and electronic equipment that were used to blow the house behind his. The place was a drug factory. Tony blew them all up. He got them all in one place and lit the bastards. Hopefully this will all end soon."

Alex walked away and headed back to the hospital to pick up his car.

He would need to call Nunzio to tell him everything that had taken place. He had to make certain that Enzo would get out of Canada and over to Sicily soon. He knew that Nick had lied to him and that if Enzo were to come back he would be incarcerated. Despite being aware of Nick's true plans, Alex would hand Tony over to the FBI. Alex had a plan, but he would not anytime soon share it with Nunzio. Getting Tony off the street would lessen the risk to all of them now. There would be some work to be done in the future to be able to get Enzo back to the states without fear of prosecution. Alex's plan would buy them the time to do just that. The timing was just right. Alex had his vacation time from the hospital scheduled for the next two weeks. It could not have come at a better time.

Alex called Nunzio at home to find that he was not there. Rosie told him that Nunzio and Stefano had rushed over to Raimondo's and Anna's house. Raimondo had called saying that Anna was ill and to please come right away. Alex drove instead to his grandparents' home. When he arrived he received the terrible news. Anna had died of a massive heart attack.

Later that evening, Stefano and Nunzio made funeral arrangements with a local funeral parlor. Afterwards, Alex and Nunzio briefly discussed Alex's meeting with the FBI agent. It was agreed that the best course of action would be to allow the FBI to get Tony off the street. Nunzio reassured Alex that Dominick would have Enzo on his way to Sicily within the next twenty- four hours. Enzo would now be safe. Alex left, telling Nunzio that he would go to Catalina's to break the news of Anna's death. "There are some other things I need to discuss with her," he told Nunzio before leaving.

TWENTY-SIX

At the last viewing, Alex was seated next to his sister. He squeezed her left hand as she wiped the tears from her eyes with the handkerchief in her right hand. Alex, himself, fought to hold back his own tears as he tried to be strong for his sister. She rested her head on his shoulder and whispered into his ear. "I hope Aunt Rita and Aunt Carina don't do that screaming and wailing like they did last night. I thought they were going to pull grandma out of her coffin."

Alex whispered back, "Sicilian funerals, quite theatrical at times, aren't they?"

"Look at Grandpa," she said. "He looks so frail and broken. It breaks my heart to see him like that."

"Sixty plus years together, that's a long time," Alex said. "Everything they have been through, my God! My guess is he won't last very long without her."

After the funeral director had recited the last prayers in the funeral home Alex turned to Enzo's friend Dominick who was seated to the right of Catalina.

"Stay with Catalina, she'll take you to the church, okay," he whispered to Dominick. Dominick nodded yes to Alex.

At the church while the pallbearers entered, the organ played Bach's "Ave Maria" as the soloist sang the words to grandma's favorite song. The congregation now seated, the priest began to recite the Mass For The Dead. The smell of incense filled the church as the clanging sound of the chain striking the incense burner echoed through the sanctuary.

Nunzio looked across the pew at Stefano. He had never seen Stefano so contrite as he appeared at that moment. Nunzio listened to the words being spoken by the priest. "Anna today finds herself in a better place; a place where she is at peace with her creator. No more will she endure the rigors of this life, but be forever present in the arms of her Lord. She is home with the angels." Nunzio wiped the tears from his eyes. He looked ahead at the crucifix on the altar. The priest continued his sermon.

"Anna will be waiting to greet each of us when we are called home by our Savior. But first we must make each of our lives right and confess our own sins so that we too may have a place in heaven and once again see our beloved Anna. God has a place reserved for each of us in his kingdom." He continued. "The scripture teaches us that none of us know the day or the hour of our passing from this life into the next. Death comes like a thief in the night. We must be ready. We must prepare our souls for the most important event in our lives. Then we will be reunited with our sister in Christ. As we now pray for the granting of rest to Anna's soul, let us also pray for the salvation of our own souls."

Nunzio was very moved by the words spoken by the priest. He reflected on his own life and the sins that he had committed. He was prepared to change his life and leave the old ways behind. He turned to Alex who was seated beside him and whispered, "We were born into this mess, we chose this life, and we now have to choose to change. We have been so blind." He took a deep breath and closed his eyes in prayer.

As Schubert's "Ave Maria," was played, Alex stared straight ahead reflecting the memories of his younger years spent with his grandparents. He examined his own life as he tried to deal with the pain he was now feeling. It was a pain that was masked in silence. Silence was the way of survival, the way of life he had come to know.

Following the funeral, family and friends gathered for a reception at a local restaurant. It was a time not only to thank those who came but to renew old acquaintances, as well. As Alex, Nunzio and Catalina made their way to each table to greet family and friends, the same words seemed to echo over and over again. "I remember when..." Soon it was time to go and family and friends left to return to their homes. Stefano informed Catalina and Alex that he would contact them in a few days so they could come over to the house and take something of Anna's as a memento of her life. Catalina left accompanied by Dominick as Alex stayed behind to spend more time with Joelle and his sons. Joelle pulled Alex aside to speak with him.

"Alex, we need to sit down and talk about the boys," she said.

"What's wrong with them?" he asked.

"There is nothing wrong with them other than they need a father full-time in their lives," she said with tears in her eyes. "They need their father to walk through the front door of their home every night and say, 'I'm home.'"

"What are you saying, Joelle?" Alex asked.

"I'm saying that it's time we set our differences aside and consider them." She fought back the tears. "They miss you, Alex."

Alex took her by the hand. "And you?" he asked. "Do you miss me?"

She looked at him for a moment and said, "It's not the same without you."

Alex pulled her close to him. They looked at each other and smiled. There was silence for a few moments.

"I've got to go away to a seminar for a few days. When I get back we'll discuss this further," Alex said to her. "There is a new day dawning for this whole family; a new beginning. Things are going to be different in this family. It's funny, we came here to mourn a death and we leave having found some new leases on life." They embraced as Alex left the restaurant. As he looked over at his sons he thought to himself, *Someday you will be great men. Men of honor and courage.*

A few days later it was time for Tony to deliver the arms to the cartel. Martin Eisman left his office in a pre-arranged limousine with two and one half million dollars in a small brown suitcase. He would meet Tony in front of the warehouse where they would walk in together to consummate the deal. The cartel members who accompanied the narcotics shipment would be waiting for Tony and Martin Eisman inside. The exchange would be made, the cartel members would have their arms and money and Tony would have his drugs.

Tony left his office and headed to the warehouse accompanied by two of his bodyguards. Martin who had a longer drive left his office earlier. The rendezvous time had been set for one o'clock in the afternoon. Tony arrived about ten minutes early and waited outside for his *consiglieri.* It was now five minutes later and Martin had not yet arrived. It was unlike Martin to ever arrive late for a meeting. Ten minutes after the hour and still no sign of Martin. Tony thought to himself, *He may be caught in traffic.* Martin would always travel unaccompanied to business meetings so not to draw any attention to an event so there was some concern on Tony's part. It was now fifteen minutes past the hour and still no sign of Martin. Tony lit a cigarette and began to pace back and forth nervously. His guests inside the building began to wonder what was going on, as well.

Tony turned to head back inside the building to inform the others that there was a slight delay. As he turned he heard a car coming around the corner. He looked up and noticed it was a limousine. "Finally," he thought to himself. As the limousine pulled up and came to a halt, Tony took one last puff of his cigarette and threw it to the ground

"It's about time," he said to Martin as he exited the vehicle. Martin appeared a bit wobbly and it took a few moments for him to regain his balance.

"What's wrong with you?" Tony asked. "Did you get car sick or something?"

Martin looked up at Tony and said, "I guess I dozed off in the car, I'm feeling a bit groggy."

"Well, wake the hell up. We've got business to conduct. You can take a snooze when we're done," Tony said to him. Martin still seemed somewhat lethargic. At that point, Tony took the small suitcase from his hands.

"Maybe you better wait out here until you feel better," Tony said. "I hope you aren't doing drugs or nothing like that."

"I don't know what the hell is wrong with me," Martin responded.

Tony carried the suitcase inside to the garage area where the other men were waiting inside.

"Gentleman, excuse me for being late," he said as he approached the others. He plopped the suitcase down on a table. At the same time, one of the others brought over a small bale of powdery substance and placed it on the table, as well. He made a small incision at the top of the package and Tony stuck his finger inside. He put his finger to his tongue, looked at the others and nodded. At that time one of the other men rolled up the door of a cube van revealing crates of weapons. Tony opened the suitcase, revealing stacks of green currency.

Suddenly, a commotion could be heard at the entrance to the garage area. In the very next instant a vehicle came crashing through the rear door of the garage area. Simultaneously, heavily armed men wearing helmets kicked in the passage doors to the garage.

"FBI! Nobody move!" one of the men shouted. Still others shouted, "Hands behind your heads! On your knees!" One of the men standing near the cargo van tried to run towards an open door. He was quickly wrestled to the ground by one of the FBI agents.

As Tony looked around he could not believe what he was seeing. He was surrounded by scores of helmeted men, wearing vests with the letters FBI and ATF. One of the agents pushed him to the ground and ordered him to put his hands behind his head. As the agent put the handcuffs around one wrist he twisted Tony's other arm to bring it down behind his back.

"Easy, damn it, easy," Tony growled. Within a matter of two minutes, the federal agents had every man in the garage handcuffed and lying face down on the ground. Tony looked around again as the federal agents now began to examine the loot of contraband in the garage. One of the agents examined the open suitcase with the currency. As he lifted a stack of bills he noticed something rather peculiar. He called out to his commander.

"Jack, come take a look at this." His commander approached the table.

"Hundred dollar bills on top, blank paper underneath," he said.

His commander looked around the room. "Any of you boys have any knowledge of this?" he asked the handcuffed men as he looked around the room. He waited for a moment and as no one had responded he then said, "No, I didn't think so." He closed the suitcase and went on his business. Tony could not believe what he had seen. *Could Martin have set him up?* he wondered. He was now assisted to his feet by one of the officers and escorted to a waiting van where he took his place next to the other handcuffed men. As he sat down he shook his head in disbelief.

At the same time that the bust at the garage was taking place, FBI agent's lead by Nick Hanson arrived at Enzo's home. While some of the agents positioned themselves around the perimeter of the house Nick accompanied by another agent banged on the front door.

"FBI! Open the door," Nick shouted as he banged on the door again. The door opened slowly.

"*Whatsa matta fu you?* A man in a sleeveless t-shirt asked as he appeared in the now open door.

"Enzo Melina, we have a warrant for your arrest," said the FBI agent.

"Enzo, Enzo, I no Enzo" the man said to the agents. The agents looked startled.

"What is your name?" asked Nick.

"Dominick, my name is Dominick," the man responded to the agents. Nick looked over to the street where one of his agents was quarreling with and attempting to detain a young woman.

"Nick, this woman claims to be Melina's daughter," yelled the agent.

"Let her go, send her up here," Nick replied. The young woman climbed the steps to the house.

"Just what the hell is going on here?" she asked.

"I'm agent Nick Hanson with the FBI. I have a warrant for the arrest of Enzo Melina. Who may you be, Miss?" asked Nick.

"I'm his daughter," she replied.

"Can you identify this man?" Nick asked, pointing to Dominick.

"Yes, I can," she responded. "This is a friend of the Melina family. His name is Dominick. Do you have a warrant for his arrest, too?" she asked.

"He bears a striking resemblance to your old man," said Nick.

She replied. "You are not the first person to make that mistake."

Nick turned to Dominick and asked, "Do you have any ID?"

"Go get your passport," Catalina said to Dominick.

Dominick went inside and returned with his passport. Nick examined it closely.

"*Itsa* okay now, *Itsa* good?" Dominick asked. Nick did not reply. Catalina stood silently by as Nick headed back down the steps.

"Shit!" he said as he headed to the waiting car. "Son-of-a-bitch!" he exclaimed.

"Get the others, let's get the hell out of here," he said to the agent who was with him. He realized he had been conned into believing that Enzo had returned from Canada to attend his mother's funeral. His surveillance team had mistaken Dominick who bore a striking resemblance to him as Enzo. While the day may have been a productive day for Nick it was by no means a total success. The Melinas had created a diversion and bought enough time to get Enzo safely off the continent.

Two days later, Nunzio called Catalina to remind her that the family would be gathering at Anna and Raimondo's house so each person could claim a memento from Anna's belongings. Since he had not heard from Alex in quite some time, he asked Catalina if she knew of his whereabouts.

"He'll be there tomorrow," Catalina responded.

The next day, the family members gathered at Anna's house. Catalina informed Nunzio and Stefano that Alex would be late and suggested that they start without him.

After the other family members had left, Catalina asked to speak to Nunzio and Stefano in private.

"What's going on sis? Is something wrong with Alex?" Nunzio asked.

"I have something I need to tell you guys," she responded. "Let's sit in the dining room." Nunzio and Stefano sat down as Catalina paced the room.

"Alex is in Europe," she said. Nunzio and Stefano looked puzzled.

"Please don't get mad at me. I helped Alex with some things last week," she said.

"Things like what?" asked Nunzio.

"When Alex met with Agent Hanson he knew that Hanson was lying to him about dad. He decided to play along and give him Tony anyhow," Catalina said. "What Alex figured was that he could get Tony off the street and not have to worry about him for a long time."

"So for this he went to Europe?" Stefano asked.

"No, let me finish," she said. "Alex knew that Tony was going to pay over two million dollars for the narcotics in addition to the shipment of arms. You all knew that, too. Alex knew how Tony operated with Martin Eisman. He knew Eisman kept Tony's money in a vault in his law offices. Eisman's M.O. was to always travel alone by limousine to these kinds meetings. He wouldn't draw any attention to himself by doing it that way." She took a sip of water out of the glass she was holding.

"Eisman would always use the same limo service to travel to the meetings. The routine was always the same. The limo would pull up in front of his office and pick him up. There was never any contact between him and the driver. The driver was given a destination and a route in advance and simply drove there. Lucky for us, Alex worked with a part-time nurse who also worked in her family's limo business. Alex got the pick up information a few days in advance and he and I worked out this plan." Catalina grinned.

"What kind of plan?" asked Nunzio.

"Alex put a latex seal around the passenger compartment of the limo where the partition was. He rigged a tube into the compartment from the trunk. He put a tank of anesthesia in the trunk and connected it to the tube. You know, the kind you inhale," she said. Nunzio and Stefano leaned forward in their seats. They could not believe what they were hearing.

"I was driving the limo that day," she said.

"What! Are you crazy? Alex put you in jeopardy like that?" Nunzio said. "This is crazy." Nunzio sprung to his feet.

"Nunzio, stop! I'm not a child. Just stop. Please! Listen," she replied.

"All right go on," he replied.

"Eisman was pretty heavily sedated by the anesthesia. I pulled over and swapped the money in the suitcase for some scrap paper with some Franklins on top," she said.

"Brilliant, just brilliant," interrupted Stefano.

"Where's the money?" asked Nunzio.

"Yeah, where is the money?" asked Stefano.

"Alex gave one hundred grand to Luigi. He told him to start a chain of sausage stands with the money. He sent another hundred to the family of some mentally retarded guy who got killed in that blast a few weeks ago." Catalina reached into her pocket took out a key and handed it to Nunzio.

"What's this?" he asked.

She responded. "It's the key to a safe deposit box at Marine Midland Bank. You'll find a million dollars there."

"*Minghia*," said Stefano.

"So you are wondering where the rest of the money is, aren't you?" she asked. "Do you remember Grandpa telling us about the Pugliese family in the old country and how they helped him out?"

"I remember," Nunzio replied.

"After the war they didn't have enough money to keep the olive groves and villa they had bought operational. It fell into disrepair. The kids and grandkids never really did anything with it." Catalina paused for a moment. "Well, Dad now has a place to live while he is hiding in Sicily."

"Unbelievable," said Stefano.

"Oh, one more thing," said Catalina. "Two more things, actually." She smiled. "Alex got the sulfur mine back, too," she said. Nunzio and Stefano silently stared at Catalina.

"Mom got a nice amount, too. She will be well taken care of now," she said.

"He stopped to see Mom?" Nunzio asked. Catalina nodded and smiled.

"So I suppose Alex told you everything about our family. He told you about dad and the business and everything else?" he asked.

She replied. "Nunzio, I may be a woman, but I'm still a part of this family. I know that all that is behind us now. The silence is now broken." She began to cry with emotion.

"He's flying to Lourdes today. He wants to stop at the grotto and pray before he comes back. He wants to ask for forgiveness and mercy for all of our souls." She continued to cry.

"He's going to call us here. I was expecting him to call over an hour ago."

Stefano heard the phone ringing in the other room. He rose from his seat to answer the phone. Nunzio and Catalina followed.

"That's probably him now," said Catalina. Stefano turned his back to Nunzio and Catalina as he continued to listen to the person talking on the other end of the line.

Catalina assumed from the lack of conversation that it was not Alex on the phone. She returned to the dining room with Nunzio and sat back down. Moments later Stefano entered the room. He had tears in his eyes and his lips were quivering.

"There's been a plane crash in the Pyrenees," he said.

Printed in the United States
31782LVS00004B/9

9 781413 754360